The McGovan Casebook

QUINTIN JARDINE is one of Britain's most successful crime writers. His acclaimed series of Edinburgh-set books based on the cases of Detective Bob Skinner includes such titles as *Fallen Gods*, *Murmuring the Judges* and *Autographs in the Rain*.

DR MARY ANNE ALBURGER, Lecturer in Music at the University of Aberdeen, is an acknowledged (and published) expert on Scottish fiddle music, and some aspects of the violin. Detective stories are an abiding interest.

James McGovan

THE McGOVAN CASEBOOK

EXPERIENCES OF A DETECTIVE IN VICTORIAN EDINBURGH

MERCAT PRESS
EDINBURGH
www.mercatpress.com

First published in 2003 by Mercat Press Ltd
10 Coates Crescent, Edinburgh EH3 7AL
www.mercatpress.com
Stories first published in *Strange Clues* (1881), *Traced and Tracked*
(1884) *and The Invisible Pickpocket* (1922)

ISBN 184183 050X

Set in Bodoni at Mercat Press
Printed and bound in Great Britain by
Antony Rowe Ltd

Contents

◉

Foreword by
Quintin Jardine

◉

IN KEEPING WITH all good novelists and short story-tellers, "James
McGovan" reaches out, takes the reader gently by the arm
and makes him a part of his world. These tales may be fictional, but the Edinburgh in which they take place is not. The
characters may be as make-believe as the Victorian detective
who describes them, but they have a veracity, and in many cases
a vivacity, about them which makes them as valid today as when
they were created a century and a quarter in the past.

McGovan's tales are colourful webs spun for the reader. They
are filled with wisdom and dark humour—take the phrase
"Calcraft's toilet" for example, a metaphor built around the public
executioner—and on occasion with absolute gems which need
no explanation even in today's complex world. "Kleptomania—
a kind of genteel name for thievery when it is committed by any
one in good society."

Although these are not histories, they are of historical value.
Most of all, though, they are high quality entertainment on the
printed page, to be read, laughed over and enjoyed.

The Mysterious Human Leg

◉

THE LEG WAS found by some boys in a backyard off the Grassmarket, and as it was wrapped in a newspaper they thought it was a piece of beef, and each wanted it all to himself. The one who ran off with it, however, and got away from all the others by his superior swiftness, had no sooner examined his prize in a safe place than he felt weak about the legs, and set it down very hastily and tottered off to get a policeman. Then the place where it had been found had to be shown, and was easily identified by some blood stains; and the leg was brought to the Central, and the boy also, for examination. It was the left leg of a man neatly taken off at the knee joint with a bevelled slash off the flesh at each side for over-lapping purposes, which plainly pointed to the hand of a practised surgeon. The cause of the amputation was also plain, for the bone had been smashed and splintered beyond repair, as if by a bullet hitting it; but what was most puzzling was the presence of some dozens of common carpet tacks which had been propelled into the flesh and had remained there. The leg appeared to have been not many hours away from its original owner, so I naturally turned to the night policeman on the beat, whom I had to rouse out of bed for the purpose. I did not expect to get a clue of any kind, but I was surprised to get a very good one. The policeman had seen a man pass out of that close about three o'clock in the morning, and he had the idea that the man was a student who was sometimes sent to people who were too poor to pay a doctor. He did not know the student's name or his address, but he described him as red haired and having a slight limp, as if one leg were shorter than the

1

other. He had spoken to the student in passing, but though he had gone into the close he had not thought of looking over a low wall into the yard where the leg was afterwards found. It seemed to me very unlikely that a student would throw away a good leg undissected, so I was doubtful of a connection, but I went out to the front of the College on chance and watched every student who entered. About one o'clock a troop of them came up from the Surgical Hospital in Infirmary Street, and I instantly spotted one who answered the description perfectly. He was a frank-faced, gentlemanly-looking fellow, and was laughing gaily with a companion when I accosted him, so I expected to have no difficulty whatever.

"You are a medical student I think, and attend cases of the poor?" I began as I drew him aside.

"Yes, sometimes," he said sobering down somewhat and summing me up on the spot as I could see.

"Were you at a case last night near the Grassmarket?" I continued.

"Are you a policeman in plain clothes?" he suddenly asked without replying to my question.

"Oh, well: something of that kind," I answered.

"Well," and he paused a little, and in the greatest good humour bestowed upon me a knowing wink, "I was not out last night at all."

I was staggered, and I must have looked the feeling for his grin became broader, and he was moving off when I suddenly held up a hand and said:—

"Are you sure?"

"Quite sure," he smilingly answered.

"And you know nothing about a lost human leg?" I continued.

"Nothing. What about it?" he answered with tantalising coolness and such widely opened eyes that I felt sure that he was laughing in his sleeve.

"Oh, nothing, except that I should like to get hold of the rest of the leg and the man at the end of it," I replied, feeling that he had the best of it. "He did not get a bullet through his bones for nothing, to say nothing of the carpet tacks. I suppose you cannot even explain the carpet tacks?"

"Quite out of my power, I assure you," he beamingly returned. "Might I ask your name?"

"M'Govan—James M'Govan," I responded, trying to look crusty, but not succeeding.

"Ah, I seem to have heard the name before—sort of detective or something, aren't you?" he airily continued. "Well, mine is Robert Manson, and I lodge in Lothian Street, No. 30. I'm rather pressed for time just now, so good-bye," and away he went quite undisturbed.

"The rascal knows all about it, but has made up his mind to keep the secret," was my thought as I watched him disappear. "However, no one has lodged a complaint as to a bullet smash or a lost leg, so things must develop a little before I can force his hand."

For some days after this failure I took to haunting the Grassmarket district after College hours in the hope of meeting Manson on a visit to the former owner of the leg, but fully a week elapsed before my wish was gratified, and then it was in a curious fashion. I was coming down the West Port at an easy pace when I heard the sound of two men in dispute near the foot of the Vennel, and I crossed the street into the shade to have a look at them, when I was surprised to find that one of them was Manson and the other a pickpocket named Pete Swift. The student was swearing at the other roundly, and telling him to be off, but a whisper from Swift seemed to pull him up, for he at length took some money from his pocket and gave it to the thief, and then moved off along the Grassmarket and vanished.

As soon as Manson was gone I crossed the street and intercepted Swift as he was moving away up the West Port.

"What have you been about now?" I sharply demanded.

"Nothing, s'elp me bob!" he protested, trying to edge past.

"You were begging—I saw you at it," I persisted.

"Begging? I never begged in my life!" he cried, looking as indignant as a clerk might look if accused of soiling his hands with manual labour. "Ye know that."

"I saw you get the money, so come along," I firmly answered, getting out the handcuffs, but he had a particular reason for disliking arrest just at that moment, and he made a bolt to get away, and, as I had to throw out the hand with the bracelets, he got an ugly bruise over the temple, which bled freely all the way to the Central, and caused him to lodge a complaint of having been treated with unnecessary violence. When he was searched, however, I began to have a dim idea of the nature of his crime, for in his breast pocket I found a letter addressed to a Mrs. Graham in Pitt Street, bearing an unobliterated stamp, and which was written in a strain not usually adopted when addressing a married woman. The letter began with "Dearest Nelly," and was signed "Your loving Bob," and was as like that of a lover address-ing his sweetheart as any letter could be. The letter appeared to have been torn open with a rough hand, and was considerably soiled through being for some time in Pete's dirty pocket. When it was brought out Pete pulled on a stagey look of surprise to convey the idea that we had placed it there by some very clever conjuring.

"Where did you get this letter?" I said. "Is it your own?"

"Blest if I ever clapped eyes on it till this minute," he sol-emnly protested. "Must 'a' fallen into my pocket out o' some winder. Them things is al'ys flyin' about." And while we laughed consumedly Pete kept on a demure look of owl-like solemnity which would have done credit to a Judge at a murder trial.

"It doesn't belong to you then?" I continued.

"Certainly not," he said with a virtuous look. "I can't write."

"You can read," I sceptically remarked, "and I think I've seen you write your name. This letter seems to have been in-tended to be posted, but perhaps was intercepted. Letter-stealing is a very serious charge."

Pete winced at the hint, and coughed uneasily.

"Then I hopes you'll get the villin that put it into my pocket," he anxiously remarked.

"Maybe we've got him already," I cheerfully responded. "Any idea who wrote it?"

Pete had an appreciation of humour when the joke came from himself; he was as dull as ditch-water when it was levelled at him, so he assumed a stolid look and said:—

"Not the least."

"It might have been written by a student," I suggestively remarked.

Pete started painfully and eyed me with great concern. "Perhaps his name is Robert Manson," I continued. Pete's face grew sickly in hue, and he asked leave to sit down—he evidently wished, now that it was too late, that he had said nothing.

"But it will be easy to find that out by asking Manson himself," I calmly added, as Pete's silence grew painful. "Perhaps it has been a case of blackmailing."

Pete still had no reply to make, and so he was marched off to the cells till I could discover what he had been about. Students are noted for keeping late hours, so I had no scruples in making direct for Manson's lodgings in Lothian Street, in which I found him comfortably seated, smoking after his supper and studying a book at the same time. He seemed quite surprised on recognising me, but quickly recovered and offered me a chair.

"You did not tell me the strict truth the other day," I casually remarked as I took the seat. "I called here immediately after and learned that you had been called out the night before to an urgent case."

"Ah, indeed!" he said, affecting to make a powerful effort at recollecting his professional engagements. "Quite possible. I have so many calls of the kind. This is my last year at College."

"You took your amputating instruments with you," I pursued, "and also some chloroform—the landlady smelt it as you went out."

"Very likely," he musingly responded. "Have a cigar?" I took the cigar, and he hastened to help me to light it.

"I suppose you did nothing wrong, that you have any interest in concealing?" I said, at last.

"Oh dear, no—a doctor can't afford to do that," he firmly answered. "I never do anything wrong."

"Indeed, then you're an exception to most men," I laughingly observed. "Is it a professional secret?"

"Hem—well—yes, something of that kind," he cautiously answered, puffing hard at the cigar; "but, to tell you the truth, I wish now I had never gone out at all that night."

"You don't say so?" I exclaimed, trying to look astonished. "After complications?"

"Well, no, not in the case—that went all right," he gloomily answered; "but I lost some papers that night, or had them taken from me, of no use to any one but the owner, of course, but still such as I should rather have in my own possession."

"Some record of experiments, no doubt," I said, helpfully.

"Em—well, no," he answered, a little in doubt of me.

"Diploma maybe?" I continued.

"Oh, bless you, no—haven't taken that yet, but expect to at the end of the session," he hastily returned.

"Accounts, maybe—or letters?" I gently insinuated.

"Em—well, yes—something of that kind," he uneasily faltered.

"Nothing that I could get hold of for you, I suppose?" I suggested.

"I'm afraid not—it's too well guarded," he gloomily answered, "but I would do anything for you if you could get it. The fact is, Mr. M'Govan, it's a love letter, and one to be understood only by the lady to whom it was addressed."

"Most love letters are of that description," I sadly observed. "I used to write them once, so I know; to the callous outsider they are pure drivel."

I waited for him to say more, but he was fidgety and suspicious, and remained silent, so at last I said:—

"Are you afraid of a breach of promise case?"

"No; a breach of peace would be more likely," he grimly answered.

"Oh!—her father object?"

"No, no—she has no father—she's an old sweetheart, that's all."

I looked at him fixedly, and then said:—

"Do you mean that she is old, or that she was once your sweetheart?

"Once my sweetheart," he answered, flushing slightly.

"And now a widow, eh?"

"N—n—no—she's not a widow yet," he slowly admitted, and he sighed drearily as if he wished she were.

I lay back and whistled aloud.

"Then you've been making love to another man's wife," I said at last.

"It would look like that to anyone who didn't under-stand," he hurriedly returned. "She and I know better."

"Imphm—they always say those things!" I dryly observed. "You seem to be in a tight place."

"Condemned tight!" he impressively rejoined, with a pain-fully troubled look. "If I once get out of this fix I'll never get into another."

"Well, I think I can help you out of the mess on two condi-tions," I quietly said at last, taking pity on him.

"Good!—I knew you were a good soul. I agree to them," he eagerly responded.

"The first is that you promise never to write to the same lady again, or to try to see her while she has a husband."

"Oh, I agree to that; it's really not safe, and scarcely right," he readily assented.

"And the second is that you tell me all about that amputation case. I have the leg, but want the other end of the man who owned it."

"And you'll get me the letter without the possibility of it reach-ing her husband?"

"I will."

"Then it's a bargain!" he said, in profoundest relief. "All I know about the business is that I was called up at one o'clock in the morning to see a man with a smashed leg. I was promised a sovereign to remain secret and the money was paid down before I started for the place. The man who came may have been a garroter or a house-breaker, for he had gallows bird written all over his face, and I took care to leave my watch and spare cash at home, and to keep one of my amputating knives open and ready in my overcoat pocket. He said the leg might have to be cut off, so I took some chloroform with me. I have been sent to several cases among the poor down in the Grassmarket and the West Port, so I suppose they knew my address through that. Well, when we got to the Grassmarket my guide asked me to let myself be blindfolded, and I consented, and I was then led, so far as I could guess, to a house in the West Port, where I found my patient lying. He was a strong man, but he was weak enough with pain and loss of blood, and I saw in a minute that the leg had to go, and gave him the chloroform with the assistance of my guide, and soon had the leg off. I made a good job of it, considering that I worked almost alone and with a bad light, and then I asked for the leg as an extra perquisite, and took it away wrapped in a newspaper and hidden under my coat. I was again blindfolded and taken back to the Grassmarket, where my guide suddenly left me. When I snatched off the bandage I guessed the cause of his haste, for not far off was the night policeman, and I ducked into a close-mouth till he should pass; but in a little he came poking along shining his lamp in on me, and I got scared and threw the leg over a wall, and walked boldly out before him and got away home."

"But what about the carpet tacks?" I asked. "The leg was full of tacks."

"I know that, or rather my best amputating knife knows it, for some of them spoiled the edge of it," he said with energy; "but the people would not explain, so I know nothing of them. He had been shot by mistake, they said, and carried home by my guide— probably while breaking into some house."

"And how did you lose the letter?"

"I never knew—I had it in my overcoat pocket ready for posting, and I may have pulled it out when I took out my amputating knife—at any rate I was stopped on the street by the same villain who took me to the place, and he demanded money, saying he would give the letter to Mrs. Graham's husband if I refused, so I caved in and gave him half a sovereign. I appealed to his sense of gratitude for all I had done for them, but it was just a waste of breath."

"And have you never again seen your patient?"

"Oh, yes, once—I was taken to him in the same way, but by a different person, and he was progressing very well. I told him of the blackmailing, and he said he would have Pete's life for it; but that did not bring back the letter or my half-sovereign. He got another out of me to-night, and will be at me again before long."

"He won't, for he's in the lock-up now," I promptly answered, "and I have the letter safe."

"You have! Give me your hand! That takes a ton weight off my mind!" he joyously exclaimed. "You might hand it over and let me burn it."

"I cannot just now, but you will get it all right later on. Now you might get on your boots and try to take me as near to your patient's lodging as you can."

He started up and got on his things, and we went down to the Grassmarket together, where I blindfolded him, and he led me up the West Port for some distance, and then stopped near a street lamp.

"Is there a close-mouth near here?" he asked, and there was, so he led me into that, and some distance down he felt for a stair on the left hand.

"It was a place like this, but I'm not sure that we are in the right close," he said, but as I knew that on that stair was living a ticket-of-leave man named Ned Cooper, I decided to go up and give him a call. The keeper of the lodging declared that Cooper had not been there for weeks, but I soon proved that she was quite mistaken, for I found him—or at least a considerable part of him—in the inner room, with a basket over his left leg to keep the bedclothes off the tender stump. As the student did not appear with me, Ned rashly jumped to the conclusion that he had been betrayed by Pete Swift, and he straightway resolved to be even with the traitor.

"It's for that crib-cracking in Lauriston, I s'pose?" he inquiringly observed; "the one that Pete Swift planned and got me to help in?"

I nodded vaguely, and Ned clenched his fists, and swore at Pete till he was black in the face.

"It'll be seven years, I s'pose?" he gloomily added, "but seeing as I was drawed into it like a innercent lamb, and was shot by the man in the house and have lost a leg, I oughter get off easier nor Pete, eh?"

"Well, it seems fair that you should, and I daresay it may be managed," I said, and as my word was as good as a bond, Ned gave me the whole particulars of the housebreaking. They had thought the house empty; but it was not, for the owner was asleep in a back room, and had emptied a gun into Ned's leg before he even sighted him. There was no pursuit, and Ned was hauled out at the open window by Pete and borne off on his back. Ned knew nothing of the finding of his leg nor of the carpet tacks with which it had been filled; so I left him under guard, and next morning called at the house into which he had broken. The owner was at breakfast alone, and he started up in manifest alarm when he recognised my face.

"Is it about the man I shot? "he faintly asked, motioning me to a chair.

I nodded, and gravely said:—

"Why did you not report the matter to us?"

"Report it? I was nearly dead with remorse, and haven't had a solid night's rest ever since," he hurriedly answered. "Is he dead?"

"Oh, no; but how did it happen?"

"Well, I'm a light sleeper, and woke with the opening of the front gate. Then I started up and listened, till I heard them trying the front parlour window. There's been a lot of housebreaking about here, so I had a gun ready loaded; but I'm no great shot, and as there was only a bullet in it, I felt pretty sure I should miss the man. On the mantlepiece, however, was a paper of tacks left by the upholsterers a few weeks ago, and I groped for that in the dark, and emptied them into the gun. I would have taken out the bullet, but I had not time, for I heard the front window being shoved up. I slipped along the lobby, and saw a man with one leg just inside the window, and I let bang at that. I think the recoil knocked me over, for when I came to again there was no sign of the man, and nothing but a great pool of blood to show what had happened. I think there were two of them, but I only saw one inside."

I laughed at the poor soul's concern and terror, and hastened to relieve his fears by stating the facts already set down. Ned Cooper was removed as soon as possible, and was able to give such information against Pete that that worthy duly got off with the anticipated seven years, while he himself got off with one. The case of the letter and the blackmailing did not appear at the trial at all, and in due time the letter was restored to Manson, who burned it before my eyes, and declared that he would never again pen another of the same kind.

A Pedlar's Revenge

◎

LATE ON A Saturday night I was coming up the North Bridge
when I saw in front of me a pedlar of cheap jewellery
tottering along with his box, singing "Champagne Charlie,"
and evidently too full of drink to think of business or hovering
hawks. By his side, and trying hard to assist him in the chorus,
was a well-known thief named Jem Wright. This rascal had his
arm hooked into that of the tipsy pedlar, while on the opposite
side of the street, and therefore within call, there hovered Jem's
consort, Bell, whose longest term had been for child-stripping—
or, to put it more correctly, for manslaughter, the poor child having
died from the stripping and exposure.

Bell was a big muscular woman; who could have overcome any
ordinary man easily, a most frightful swearer, and remorseless as
the grave; Jem was a slightly-built fellow, below medium height,
and not nearly so debased, but completely in awe of his consort.

The pedlar, in the exuberance of his glee occasionally waved
his right hand in the air, and as that hand held the leather handle
of the brass-bound box containing his stock, it struck me at a
glance that the contents might be the cause of Jem's affectionate
regards. The pedlar himself was unknown to me, and therefore
probably a stranger in the city, but he was well enough clothed
and booted to suggest that his box might be worth emptying.

"Look here, my man," I said, getting alongside, and thus
suddenly chilling down Jem Wright's vocal efforts, "do you know
the fellow you're walking with?"

The pedlar paused and blinked at me hazily, and then rapidly
began to lose his temper.

12

"Peffly well, sir," he thickly answered, with an attempt at a severe frown. "S—s—s my frien'—my frien', sir, and I'd thank you to min' your own business, sir."

At the same moment he received a cautioning dig in the ribs from the elbow of Wright, but the warning came too late, and was scarcely understood even then.

"I am just doing that," I coolly answered. "You've a licence, I suppose?—let me see it."

He took his box in the other hand, and at length, with much difficulty, produced the required paper from his breast pocket, from which I learned that John M'Coll, Glasgow, was duly licensed to sell the articles he carried.

"You are John M'Coll, I suppose?"

"That's me—Jake M'Coll," he promptly answered.

"Well then, M'Coll, the man you are with is a thief, so take care of yourself."

"A thief?" he hazily responded; then he slowly turned to Wright and said sternly—"You be off."

"What?" exclaimed Wright, in aggrieved surprise.

"You be off!" I sternly commanded, and without another word he slunk off, and disappeared up the street, to join his consort, still hovering in the distance.

I accompanied M'Coll as far as the High Street, during which short walk he assured me repeatedly that he was quite able to take care of himself against all the Edinburgh keelies in existence, and that he knew his way to the lodging-house he occupied, and considered my offer of a policeman to conduct him as nothing short of an insult. We then parted, and I saw him no more till next morning. But he was heard of before that time. About an hour after I had left him he was found lying at the bottom of Lyon's Close, nearly senseless, and as he smelled strongly of drink he was bundled off to the Central as a simple "drunk." His box, however, was found lying near him, and as the lid had been forced open, and a drawer below pulled out and left empty, it was thought possible that there might have been a robbery. One of the most unaccountable circumstances of the case was that a bank book representing about £20 to M'Coll's credit had been left on the ground beside the empty box.

In the morning M'Coll felt very much the worse for his drink, and the blow, which had raised a lump as big as a bap on the top of his head, and the hard bed and wooden pillow, but he was able to ask for his box, and no sooner saw it than he exclaimed that he had been robbed, and demanded particulars. Much to his annoyance no one could give them; and naturally he himself was appealed to to supply the facts. Then he got furious, and declared that he remembered nothing, and asked that detectives should at once be sent to scour the city for his stock of cheap jewellery. When I arrived I went down to see him, but he had no recollection of me or of our meeting the night before, and when it was described to him he only broke out into the bitterest reproaches against me.

"You saw that I was in danger of being robbed, and yet you left me to their mercy! What is police for if they're not to protect us?" and then he swore for about five minutes on end to relieve himself, after which I explained that I had wished to protect him, but that be insolently refused an escort.

"Tut; I was drunk—you should not have heeded what I said," he unreasonably rejoined. "You ought to have taken me up and locked me in a cell, box and all. That was your duty, and you did not do it."

It was but a waste of time to attempt to reason with such a being, so I hastened to ask him if he knew anything of "his friend," Jem Wright, and was not surprised to learn that he had no recollection of having met the man.

"I think I can get the two who did the robbery," I remarked, in hope of stopping his shower of abuse; "but the stuff itself is probably scattered or melted long ago. It should be a lesson to you to protect yourself by taking no drink."

The remark was so much breath wasted. He could not see that the fault was his own, and declared that if I did not get the

plunder as well as the thieves he would "make it hot for me"—
a threat so common that it neither depressed nor annoyed me.

After all, the prize had not been a great one. According to
his own admission the stuff taken from the box could all have
been bought for £15, and that, with his silver watch, which had
vanished with it, would probably not bring the thieves a third of
its value. M'Coll was somewhat mollified by the restoration of
his bank book, but he was impatient to see me off after the
thieves, and I left him to search for Jem and Bell. These two
had lodged with an Irishwoman in Carrubber's Close, and I
went to the house first, but failed to find them. They had not
been in the place for twenty-four hours at least, which looked
like flight, and therefore tended to link them with the crime. In
truth I was astonished that they should have set on the pedlar,
after being seen by me in his company, as they must have known
that whenever the case was reported I should be after them,
and till that moment I had half a suspicion that some other had
taken the victim up after the Wrights were chased off by me.
There was another reason in favour of this theory—the throwing
away of the bank book. Both Jem and Bell could read, and
would not have thrown away a bank book if they had thought it
possible to get the money which it represented, and the act
seemed more like that of a person who could not read. That
was my idea at the time, but I changed it after. I heard nothing
of the Wrights that day, though I made it pretty certain that
none of the plunder was concealed about the house in which
they had lodged; but next day I came upon them both by the
merest chance down at the Waverley Station in the act of taking
out third-class tickets for Dundee. They ungratefully turned
their backs on me the moment I appeared, but I made my presence known to them by getting between them and turning them
round by the shoulders to face me.

"You must have known I was looking for you," I reproachfully remarked, but Jem's reply was unfit for publication, while
Bell turned on me with a storm of language strong enough to

have sunk the island. She even looked as if half inclined to use
her fists or claws as well, but I merely waved her off, saying:—

"That'll do. You may bully your husband, but don't imagine
you can frighten me."

She seemed to think the advice good, for she heaped her
language upon Jem all the way to the Office in a style that suggested that the possession of her was not an unmixed blessing.
Jem, however, meekly held his tongue; the events soon proved
that his was the wiser course. There was nothing in their possession to connect them with the robbery.

They had a little money, but there was not a trace of the
pedlar's jewellery or his silver watch. When they were placed
before M'Coll he failed to identify them as his assailants. Indeed
he had no recollection of being knocked down or robbed, and
though he was bitter enough against the pair when he learned
that none of his property had been got with them, he was still
truthful enough to go no further than his memory. We kept the
precious pair for a short time, and then were compelled to let
them go. M'Coll was furious, and most of his wrath was directed
against me.

"You wanted them to get off," he recklessly cried, letting out
some swearing almost as strong as if it had been shaped by Bell's
sweet lips. "They've paid you well, and you've let them slip."

"On the contrary, I should have liked very much to have got
that fiend of a woman in for seven or ten years," I replied, with
astonishing calmness; and then I told him of the child stripping
case and the light punishment which Bell had suffered for her
crime. The relation only incensed M'Coll the more.

"She's an unhanged murderer," he exclaimed, "and yet you
allow her to go free after nearly murdering me as well. Such
wretches would be better dead, or at least in prison, out of harm's
way, yet you won't take them."

"If you can swear that they attacked and robbed you we will
very soon put them out of harm's way," I retorted; but he could
not do that. He said we could not expect him to do our work, and

altogether seemed as unreasonable as the woman who cried herself to death because she could not breakfast off her husband's
nose. He was surprised, as I had been, at the thieves leaving
him his bank book, but I explained that the money could only
have been got by the forgery of his signature, and that Jem and
Bell were probably afraid to risk twenty years for as many pounds.

"And then," I cheerfully added, "they probably guessed that
you would draw the money yourself to restock your box, and that
you would then get drunk again, when they could rob you as
easily as before. Bell is a knowing one, and Jem is not far behind
her."

"Me? Rob me? Never in this world," he firmly returned. "I'll
never get drunk as long as I live."

"Oh, yes you will," I as confidently returned, "and from a
remark of Bell's, I don't think they mean to lose sight of you.
Such a fool as you is not to be picked up every day."

The stab evidently went home, for he sat silent and grim for
some moments.

"They'll never rob me," he said at last, with more determination than ever; "if they try it they'll suffer for it—that's all. But
I'll tell you what I'll do—I'll try to find out if they really are the
ones who robbed me, and I'll put them into your hands as neat as
ninepence."

"You'll be clever, if you do," I said derisively, for I now saw
that this pig-headed pedlar could be managed best, as some
husbands are managed, by apparent opposition. "Jem is a wary
customer, and Bell is about as dangerous as a hungry tiger in a
lonely wood."

"I am clever," he doggedly answered, "and I will do them."

"When you have done it, you can come and let me know all
about it," I smilingly retorted; and thus we parted, the pedlar
scowling darkly.

Whether my caustic words had roused him to action, or the
whole was but the result of his own vindictive mind I cannot tell,
but after a night's thinking M'Coll went down to the lodging in

Carrubber's Close, and found there both Jem and Bell, to whom he made the following queer proposal:—

"I know perfectly well that you emptied my box after knocking me on the head," he boldly remarked, "but seeing that the police could not bring it home to you, I'm willing to strike a bargain with you on my own account. I've got some money in the bank," and just then he noticed that Jem and Bell grinned significantly to each other, "and if you'll give me back the things you took from the box and my silver watch, I'll pay you ten pounds down, as they'll cost me more to buy."

Alas! the Wrights would have been only too glad to close with the offer, but the plunder was already sold for about half the sum offered, and the money all gone. They therefore made a virtue of necessity, and most solemnly asserted that they were not the thieves who had attacked him, but held out a vague hope that they might be able to discover those dastardly wretches for him if he were prepared to pay them for the work and fee them in advance.

To this tempting proposal the pedlar appeared to listen with great eagerness, and then in a burst of confidence he told them that he could not fee them just then, as he had not yet drawn the money, but that he would get it next day at a certain hour, when he intended restocking his box. If he had any money over after the stocking had been completed, he declared that he would, in the evening, visit them, and fee them to ferret out the wretches who had wronged him. The moment the pedlar was out of the house Jem and Bell rubbed their hands and chuckled in great glee over his simplicity, and the moment M'Coll himself was outside the room he rubbed his hands and chuckled over their simplicity. We are busy doing that all the world over. The Wrights thought M'Coll a simpleton for revealing his plans to them, while the truth is that the success of his plan depended upon them knowing all about his movements. It was simply a case of diamond cut diamond, and their mistake was the common one of thinking that a man with a stupid face cannot be a perfect fox in cunning.

On the forenoon of the next day M'Coll left his lodging with his empty box in his hand, and went, as he had promised, and drew the £20. He appeared to see nothing, but was perfectly conscious that he was watched and followed by the Wrights, and, had the time been night instead of day, and M'Coll top heavy with drink, they would have attacked him before he could turn the good money into trashy jewellery, which no reset would look at without a grumble. If M'Coll had aimed only at bringing the pair to justice he would probably have adopted some such mode of luring them into a trap, but it was not justice he longed for, but revenge. The lump on his head, which had been inflicted with the heel of Bell's boot for want of a better weapon, had not quite subsided, and caused him to groan every time he put his hat on, and his plan was to give the two as much pain as he had suffered through them. He therefore wandered on, apparently unconscious of their presence, till he came to a Birmingham warehouse on the South Bridge, at which he got his box stocked. This box was bound with brass and fitted with a lock, but the lock was only in use when he slept, two belts and a leather handle between sufficing for use during his daily tours through the city. The lower half of the box was a deep drawer, fitted with trays on which he kept the better class of jewellery. The drawer could be fastened by passing an iron wire down through the end of the box from above before closing the upper part, but it usually was fastened only with a spring, for ready access by day. After having his box filled M'Coll took a few streets of houses, and did a little business on his way back to his lodging, just to show his followers that there was something in the box worth taking. Among other shops which he entered in this way was an ironmonger's in the High Street, where he appeared to have been rather a buyer than a seller, for when he reappeared he carried a parcel under his arm about the size of three pounds of sugar, the contents of which the Wrights roughly set down as cheap pocket-knives to be sold over again. What delighted them most was the fact that M'Coll entered several public-houses, and remained in them for some time, thus

giving hope of a delightful stupor of drunkenness before night-
fall. After leaving the ironmonger's M'Coll crossed the street to
his lodging and had dinner, after which he remained shut in his
own room for a considerable time, making alterations in his box.
He first took out the jewellery and locked it in his trunk; then he
carefully removed the partition separating the upper part from
the drawer below, and glued some matches to the side of the
drawer with their heads pressed hard against a piece of emery-
cloth also glued to the box. As soon as these were dry and firm,
he filled the drawer with gunpowder which he had bought in the
ironmonger's, considerately adding to that several iron nuts and
bits of lead and a packet of old nails which he had got from his
landlady. That done, he replaced the partition, filled up the top
with pads of brown paper, and glued down and locked the lid. He
then had a box of jewels ready for any thief who cared to take
them by force, and enjoyed himself till dark by noting occasionally from the window that his watchers were still devotedly waiting in the street below. He had already told them that his best
time for business was after dark about the flashy public-houses,
and they doubtless were longing for him to set out on his evening
tour. Jem and Bell relieved each other in the watching, but at
length their anxiety was ended by M'Coll appearing with his jewel
box, and making straight for their lodging.

"He's going to give us some money before he starts, in case
he should spend it all before he gets back," was their joyful
comment, and they hurried after him with such alacrity that
M'Coll had no sooner been told that they were out than they
appeared at his side and invited him in. His visit was not a prolonged one, for he had only to tell them that his box was re-
stocked, and that he hoped to draw as much money that night as
to be able to pay them five shillings of a fee in the morning. They
pressed him to take some whisky—with laudanum in it—but he
declined on the plea that he had taken too much already, and so
left them. M'Coll was careful not to look back, but was quite
certain that he was followed by Jem and Bell. His calls were

mostly to public-houses, and it delighted his followers to note that
he left every one of these with a gait decidedly more unsteady,
and a tendency to burst into song and wave his disengaged arm in
the air. Their intention was to wait till he was thoroughly stupefied,
and the hour much later, when they could easily knock him down
and run off with his box, but a moment's seeming thoughtlessness
on his part was too great a temptation to be resisted. M'Coll had
been staggering along the South Bridge apparently gloriously happy
with the drink which they imagined he had swallowed, when an
insane idea that he could light his pipe appeared to seize him, for
he set down his box on the pavement and struck match after match,
which were as speedily blown out by the wind. Then a bright idea
seemed to strike him, and he stepped into an entry close by, to be
out of the wind, foolishly leaving his box on the ground.

"There's the chance!—take it now!" whispered Bell.

"No; it's too risky," said Jem, hanging back.

He was right, as I have shown; but when was there a wife who
did not know better than her husband? She kicked him aside as a
useless encumbrance, darted at the box like a hawk at a pigeon, and
swiftly ran for the next entry, followed by her corrected husband.

The moment they were within the entry, the lower stair of
which ran down to Niddry Street, Bell tried to wrench open the
lid of the box, but found it fast.

"Watch the entry mouth while I empty the box," she resolutely commanded. One must always lead in the world, and when
a husband fails of course the wife must take command. Bell darted
down a step or two, and was speedily convinced that the lid of
the box was too strongly fastened down for even her strong hands,
and hastily made a powerful wrench at the handle of the drawer.
Instantly there was an explosion which, in that empty stair and
entry, sounded like the one o'clock gun. Bell had emptied the
box most effectually, but the most of it went into her own body
instead of her pockets. The box had ceased to be a box, and Bell
had almost ceased to be a woman. What was left of her, however,
was alive, though bleeding rapidly and frightfully burnt; so when

Jem ran in to see what was wrong he had only half a wife to lift in his arms. A policeman and some others, including M'Coll, followed him, and as his face was bleeding profusely from an iron cut which had ploughed its way along his cheek they demanded an explanation. He had none to give, and was promptly collared and handcuffed as a wife murderer, while Bell was lifted and borne on a shawl along to the Infirmary. Jem himself became so faint with loss of blood that they decided to take him to the Infirmary also. M'Coll had at first made up his mind to say nothing, but as the brass plate from the lid of the box bearing his name was found among the wreck he thought better of it.

I stopped along there to light my pipe," he exclaimed, "and I wasn't a minute about it when I missed my box and heard the noise. I suppose some powder which I had in it had gone off in their hands. I meant to carry a pistol, you know, as I was robbed a short time ago."

Jem heard the explanation as it was thus innocently tendered to the policeman, and showed his distrust and scepticism by faintly trying to get at the pedlar's throat with his clutching fingers, but being too weak he only dropped on the other side, and was picked up and carried after the half of his wife that wasn't scattered about the stair. At the Infirmary they could do nothing for Bell but see her die, and as she was a powerfully built woman, and life did not leave her easily, they thought best to let Jem know of what was about to happen. He was sitting in another ward with his cheek sewed up and a great many bandages above the sewing when the house surgeon gravely appeared before him uncertain how to break the awful news.

"That woman is your wife, I believe?" he at length found courage to say.

"Yes," said Jem, rousing slightly and peering eagerly out of the bandages, "she's pretty badly hurt, ain't she?" he added with some eagerness.

"Yes. You must bear up, my poor fellow, you must bear up," said the sympathetic surgeon, laying his hand on his shoulder, "for I have something serious to tell you." Jem started, and on the small patch of brow visible little beads of cold sweat began to break out.

"What—what is it?" he fearfully gasped, "They said—they said she was bound to go—they said so."

"Yes, she is beyond hope," was the grave reply, the truth being that Bell was already gone.

"Oh, is that it?" said Jem, evidently profoundly relieved and wiping the cold sweat from the patch of brow, "I thought you meant she was to get better." O, ingratitude, thy name is husband!

No one shed a tear for the dead child-stripper, and even Jem went to prison for nine months with a light heart, because he knew that she would not be at the prison gate to welcome him when his term was over. M'Coll's story of the powder in his box was so plausible that it was accepted without suspicion, and he himself was commended by the Judge for the manner in which he gave his evidence, and I got the truth out of him long after when I found him in a whiskified condition in a public-house down in Greenside.

The Murdered Tailor's Watch

(A Curiosity in Circumstantial Evidence)

◉

T HE CASE OF the tailor, Peter Anderson, who was beaten to
death near the Royal Terrace, on the Calton Hill, may not
yet be quite forgotten by some, but, as the after-results
are not so well known, it will bear repeating.

Some working men, hurrying along a little before six in the
morning, found Anderson's body in a very steep path on the hill,
and in a short time a stretcher was got and it was conveyed to
the Head Office. The first thing I noticed when I saw the body
was that one of the trousers' pockets was half-turned out, as if
with a violent wrench, or a hand too full of money to get easily
out again; and from this sprang another discovery—that the
waistcoat button-hole in which the link of his albert had evidently been constantly worn was wrenched clean through. There
was no watch or chain visible, and the trousers' pockets were
empty, so the first deduction was clear—the man had been robbed.

Robbery, indeed, appeared to me, at this stage of the case, to
have been the prime cause of the outrage, and an examination of
the body confirmed the idea. The neck was not broken, but there
were marks of a strangulating arm about the neck, and the inju-
ries about the head were quite sufficient to cause death. These
seemed to indicate that two persons had been engaged in the
crime, as is common in garroting cases—one to strangle and
the other to rob and beat—and made me more hopeful of track-
ing the doers. On examining the spot at which the body had been
found, I found traces of a violent struggle, and also a couple of
folded papers, which proved to be unreceipted accounts headed

"Peter Anderson, tailor and clothier," with the address of his place of business. These might have given us a clue to his identity had such been needed, but his wife had been at the Office reporting his absence only an hour before his body was brought in, and we had only to turn to her description of his person and clothing to confirm our suspicion.

Anderson, on the fatal night on which he disappeared, had unexpectedly drawn an account of some £10 or £12 from a customer, and in the joy of receiving the money had invited the man to an adjoining public-house to drink "a jorum," and one round followed another until poor Peter Anderson's head was fitter for his pillow than for guiding his feet. On entering the public-house— which was a very busy one, not far from the Calton Hill— Anderson, I found, had gone up to the bar, and before all the loungers or hangers-on pulled a handful of notes, and silver, and gold from his trousers' pocket, saying to his companion:—

"What will you have?"

Afterwards, when they got into talk, they adjourned to a private box at the back; but it was there I thought that the mischief had been done. Anderson had a gold albert across his breast, and might be believed to have a watch at the end of it; but the chain, after all, might have been only plated, and the watch a pinchbeck thing, to a thief not worth taking; but the reckless display of a handful of notes, gold, and silver, if genuine criminals chanced to see it, was a temptation and revelation too powerful to be resisted. The man who carried money in that fashion was likely to have more in his pockets, and a gold watch at least. If he got drunk, or was likely to get drunk, he would be worth waiting and watching for; so, at least, I thought the intending criminals would reason, never dreaming of course of the plan ending in determined resistance and red-handed murder. Your garroter is generally a big coward, and will never risk his skin or his liberty with a sober man if he can get one comfortably muddled with drink.

There was no time to elaborate theories or schemes of capture. A gold watch and chain valued at about £30 and £14 in money, were gone. A rare prize was afloat among the sharks, and I surmised that the circumstance would be difficult to hide. The thief and the honest man are alike in one failing—they find it difficult to conceal success. It prints itself in their faces; in the quantity of drink they consume; in the tread of their feet; the triumphant leer at the baffled or sniffing detective, and in their reckless indulgence in gaudy articles of flash dress. I went down to the Cowgate and Canongate at once, strolling into every likely place, and nipping up quite a host of my "bairns." I thought I had got the right men indeed when I found two known as "The Crab Apple" and "Coskey" flush of money and muddled with drink, but a day's investigation proved that they owed their good fortune to a stupid swell who had got in to their clutches over in the New Town. Coskey, indeed, strongly declared that he did not believe the Anderson affair had been managed by a professional criminal at all.

"If it had been done by any of us I'd have heard on it," was his frank remark to me.

I was pretty sure that Coskey spoke the truth, for in his nervous anxiety to escape Calcraft's toilet* he had actually confessed to me all the particulars of the New Town robbery by which his own pockets had been filled, and which afterwards led to a seven years' retirement from the scene of his labours.

The hint thus received prepared me for making the worst slip of all I had made in the case. I went to Anderson's widow to get the number of the watch, and some description by which it might be identified. She could not tell me the number or the maker's name; she could only say that it had a white dial and black figures, but declared that she would know it out of a thousand by a deep "clour" or indentation on the back of the case.

"I was there when it got the mark," she said, "and I could never be mistaken if the watch was put before me. A thief might alter the number, but nobody could take out that mark, for we tried it, and the watchmaker could do nothing for it. My man was working hard one day with the watch on, when a customer called

---

* William Calcraft served as official hangman from 1829 to 1874

to be measured. The waistcoat he wore wasn't a very bonny one, and he whipped it off in a hurry, forgetting about the watch, which was tugged out, and came bang against the handle of one of his irons. The watch was never a bit the worse, but the case had aye the mark on it—just there," and the widow, to illustrate her statement, showed me a spot on the back of my own watch, and then so minutely explained the line of the indentation, its length and its depth, that I felt sure that if it came in my way I should be able to identify it as readily as by a number.

This would have been all very well if her information had there ended, but it didn't.

"You are hunting away among thieves and jail birds for the man that did it," she bitterly remarked, "but I think I could put my hand on him without any detective to help me."

"You suspect someone, then?" I exclaimed, with a new interest.

"Suspect? I wish I was as sure of anything," she answered, with great emphasis. "The brute threatened to do it."

"What brute?"

"Just John Burge, the man who was working to him as journeyman two months ago."

"Indeed. Did they quarrel?"

"A drunken passionate wretch that nobody would have any thing to do wi'," vehemently continued the widow, waxing hotter in her words with every word she had uttered, "but just because they had been apprentices together Peter took pity on him and gave him work. They were aye quarrelling, but one day it got worse than usual, and I thought my man would have killed him. It was quite a simple thing began it—an argument as to which is the first day in summer—but in the end they were near fighting, and after Peter had near choked him, Burge swore that he would have his life for it—that he would watch him night and day, and then knock the sowl oot o' him in some dark corner, before he knew where he was.' That was after the master and the laddies had thrown him out at the door and down the stair; and for some days I wouldn't let Peter cross the door. But he only laughed at me after a bit, and said that Burge's 'bark was waur than his bite;' and went about just as usual. And all the time the wicked, ungrateful wretch was watching for a chance to take his life."

"Why did you not tell us of this quarrel at first?" I asked, after a pause.

"Because I thought you detectives were so sharp and clever that you would have Burge in your grips before night, without a word from me; but you're not nearly so clever as you're called."

"But he never actually attacked your husband?" I quietly interposed, knowing that wives are apt to take exceedingly exaggerated views of their husband's wrongs or rights.

"Oh, but he did, though. He came up once, not long after the quarrel, and said he had not got all the money due to him, and tried to murder Peter with the cutting shears."

"Murder him? How could he murder him with shears?" I asked, with marked scepticism.

"Well, I didn't wait to see; but ran in and gripped him by the arms till my man took the shears from him. The creatur' had no more strength than a sparry, though he's as tall as you."

"No more strength than a sparrow?" That incidental revelation staggered me. It seemed to me quite impossible that a weak man could have been the murderer of Anderson, unless, indeed, he had had an accomplice, and that was unlikely with a man seeking mere revenge. For a moment I was inclined to think it possible that Burge might have tracked his victim to the hill and accomplished the revenge, and that afterwards, when he had fled the spot, some of the "ghosts" haunting the hill might have stripped the dead or dying man of his valuables; but several circumstances led me to reject the supposition—wisely, too, as it appeared in the end. Burge, the widow told me, was a tall man, with a white, "potty" face, and a little, red, snub-nose, and always wore a black frock coat and dress hat. I took down the name of the street in which he lived—for I could get no number—and turned in that direction. In about fifteen minutes I had reached, not the street, but the crossing leading to it, when I met full in the face a man answering his description, and having the unmistakable tailor's "nick" in his back.

"That should be Burge," was my mental conclusion, though I had never seen him before. "If he's not, he is at least a tailor, and may know him," and then I stopped him with the words—

"Do you know a tailor called John Burge who lives here- about?"

"That's me," he said, with sudden animation, taking the pipe from his mouth, and evidently expecting a call at his trade, "who wants me?"

"I do."

"Oh," and he looked me all over, evidently wondering how I looked so unlike the trade.

There was a queer pause, and then I said—

"My name's M'Govan, and I want you to go with me as far as the Police Office, about that affair on the Calton Hill."

A wonderful change took place in his face the moment I uttered the words—a change which, but for the grave nature of the case, would have been actually comical; his "potty" white cheeks became red, and his red snub-nose as suddenly became white.

"Well, do you know, that's curious!" he at length gasped; "but I was just coming up to the Office now, in case I should be suspected of having a hand in it. I had a quarrel with Anderson, and said some strong things, I've no doubt, in my passion, but of course I never meant them."

I listened in silence; but my mental comment, I remember, was, "A very likely story!"

"I was coming up to say what I can prove—that I was at the other end of the town that night, and home and in my bed by a quarter to eleven," he desperately added, rightly interpreting my silence.

I became more interested at the mention of the exact hour; for I had ascertained beyond doubt that Anderson had not left the public-house and parted with his friend till eleven o'clock struck. He had, in fact, been "warned out," along with a number of bar-loafers, at shutting-up time.

"Did any one see you at home at that hour?" I asked, after cautioning him.

"Yes, the wife and bairns."

"Imphm."

"You think that's not good evidence; but I have more; I was in a public-house with some friends till half-past ten; they can swear to that; and they went nearly all the road home with me," he continued with growing excitement "Do I look like a murderer? My God! I could swear on a Bible that such a thing was never in my mind. Don't look so horrible and solemn, man, but say you believe me."

I couldn't say that, for I believed the whole a fabrication got up in a moment of desperation; and little more was spoken on either side till we reached the Head Office, where he repeated the same story to the Fiscal, and was locked up. I fully expected that I should easily tear his story to pieces by taking his so-called witnesses one by one, but I was mistaken. His wife and children, for example, the least reliable of his witnesses in the eyes of the law, became the strongest, for when I called and saw them they were in perfect ignorance both of Burge's arrest and the fact that he expected to be suspected.

They distinctly remembered their father being home "earlier" on that Friday night, and the wife added that it was more than she had expected, for by being in bed so early Burge had been able to rise early on the following morning and finish some work on the Saturday which she had fully expected would be "disappointed." Then the men with whom he had been drinking and playing dominoes up to half-past ten were emphatic in their statements, which tallied almost to a minute with those of Burge. Burge had not been particularly flush of money after that date, but, on the contrary, had pleaded so hard for payment of the work done on the Saturday that the man was glad to compromise matters and get rid of him by part payment in shape of half-a-crown. The evidence, as was afterwards remarked, was not, the best—a few drinkers in a public-house, whose ideas of 'time and place might be readily believed to be hazy, and the interested wife and children of the suspected man; but in the absence of condemning facts it sufficed, and after a brief detention Burge was set at liberty.

About that time, among the batch of suspected persons in our keeping was a man named Daniel O'Doyle. How he came to be suspected I forget, but I believe it was through having a deal of silver and some sovereigns in the pockets of his ragged trousers when he was brought to the Office as a "drunk and disorderly." O'Doyle gave a false name, too, when he came to his senses; but then it was too late, for a badly-written letter from some one in Ireland had been found in his pocket when he was brought in. He was a powerfully-built man, and in his infuriated state it took four men to get him to the Office. He could give no very satisfactory account of how he came by the money in his possession. He had been harvesting, he said, but did not know the name of the place or its geographical position, except that it was east of Edinburgh "a long way," and he was going back to Ireland with his earnings, but chanced to take a drop too much and half-murder a man in Leith Walk, and so got into our hands. On the day after his capture and that of his remand O'Doyle was "in the horrors," and at night during a troubled sleep was heard by a man in the same cell to mutter something about "Starr Road," and having "hidden it safe there." This brief and unintelligible snatch was repeated to me next morning, but, stupid as it now appears to me, I could make nothing of it. I knew that there was no such place as "Starr Road" in Edinburgh, and said so; and as for him having hidden something, that was nothing for a wandering shearer, and might, after all, be only his reaping hook or bundle of lively linen. O'Doyle was accordingly tried for assault, and sentenced to thirty days' imprisonment, at the expiry of which he was set at liberty and at once disappeared. My impression now is that O'Doyle was never seriously suspected of having had a hand in the Calton Hill affair, but that, being in our keeping about the time, he came in for his share of suspicion among dozens more perfectly innocent. If he had had bank-notes about him it might have been different, for I have found that there is a strong feeling against these and in favour of gold among the untutored Irish, which induces them to get rid of them almost as soon as they chance to receive them.

So the months passed away and no discovery was made; we got our due share of abuse from the public; and the affair promised to remain as dark and mysterious as the Slater murder in the Queen's Park. But for the incident I am now coming to, I believe the crime would have been still unsolved.

About two years after, I chanced to be among a crowd at a political hustings in Parliament Square, at which I remember Adam Black came in for a great deal of howling and abuse. I was there, of course, on business, fully expecting to nip up some of my diligent "family" at work among the pockets of the excited voters; but no game could have been further from my thoughts than that which I had the good fortune to bag. I was moving about on the outskirts of the crowd, when a face came within the line of my vision which was familiar yet puzzling. The man had a healthy prosperous look, and nodded smilingly to me, more as a superior than an inferior in position.

"Don't you remember me?—John Burge; I was in the Anderson murder, you mind; the Calton Hill affair;" and then I smiled too and shook the proffered hand.

"How are you getting on now?"

"Oh, first rate—doing well for myself;" was the bright and pleased-looking answer. "Yon affair was a lesson to me; turned teetot. when I came out, and have never broke it since. It's the best way."

It seemed so, to look at him. The "potty" look was gone from his face; his cheeks had a healthy colour, and his nose had lost its rosiness. His dress too was better. The glossy, well-ironed dress hat was replaced by one shining as if fresh from the maker, and the threadbare frock coat by one of smooth, firm broadcloth. He was getting stouter, too, and his broad, white waistcoat showed a pretentious expanse of gold chain. He chatted away for some time, evidently a little vain of the change in his circumstances, and at length drew out a handsome gold watch, making, as his excuse for referring to it, the remark—

"Ah, it's getting late; I can't stay any longer."

My eye fell upon the watch, as it had evidently been intended that it should, and almost with the first glance I noticed a deep nick in the edge of the case, at the back. Possibly the man's own words had taken my mind back to the lost watch of the murdered tailor and its description, but certainly the moment I saw the mark on the case I put out my hand with affected carelessness, as he was slipping it back to his pocket, saying—

"That's a nice watch; let's have a look at it."

It was tendered at once, and I found it to have a white china dial and black figures. At last I came back to the nick and scrutinised it closely.

"You've given it a bash there," I remarked, after a pause.

"No, that was done when I got it."

"Bought it lately?"

"Oh, no; a long time ago."

"Who from?"

"From one of the men working under me; I got it a great bargain," he answered with animation. "It's a chronometer, and belonged to an uncle of his, but it was out of order—had lain in the bottom of a sea chest till some of the works were rusty—and so I got it cheap."

"Imphm. There has been some lying in the bargain anyhow," I said, after another look at the watch, "for it is an ordinary English lever, not a chronometer. Is the man with you yet?"

"No; but, good gracious! you don't mean to say that there's anything wrong about the watch? It's not—not a stolen one?"

"I don't know, but there was one exactly like this stolen that time that Anderson was killed."

In one swift flash of alarm, his face, before so rosy, became as white as the waistcoat covering his breast.

Then he slowly examined the watch with a trembling hand and finally stammered out—

"I remember it, and this is not unlike it. But that's nothing—hundreds of watches are as like as peas."

I differed with him there, and finally got him to go with me to the Office, at which he was detained, while I went in search of Anderson's widow to see what she would say about the watch.

If I had an opinion at all about the case at this stage, it was that the watch taken was not that of the murdered man. I could scarcely otherwise account for Burge's demeanour. He appeared so surprised and innocent, whereas a man thus detected in the act of wearing such a thing, knowing its terrible history, could scarcely have helped betraying his guilt.

My fear, then, as I made my way to the house of Anderson's widow, was that she, woman-like, would no sooner see the mark on the case than she would hastily declare it to be the missing watch. To avoid as far as possible a miscarriage of justice, I left the watch at the Office, carefully mixed up with a dozen or two more then in our keeping, one or two of which resembled it in appearance. I found the widow easily enough, and took her to the Office with me, saying simply that we had a number of watches which she might look at, with the possibility of finding that of her husband. The watches were laid out before her in a row, faces upward, and she slowly went over them with her eye, touching none till she came to that taken from Burge. Then she paused, and there was a moment's breathless stillness in the room.

"This ane's awfu' like it," she said, and, lifting the watch, she turned it, and beamed out in delight as she recognised the sharp nick on the back of the case. "Yes, it's it! Look at the mark I told you about."

She pointed out other trifling particulars confirming the identity, but practically the whole depended on exactly what had first drawn my attention to the watch—the nick on the case. Now dozens of watches might have such a mark upon them, and it was necessary to have a much more reliable proof before we could hope for a conviction against Burge on such a charge.

I had thought of this all the way to and from the widow's house. She knew neither the number of the watch nor the maker's name, but with something like hopefulness I found that she knew the name of the watchmaker in Glasgow who had sold it to her husband, and another in Edinburgh who had cleaned it. I went through to Glasgow the same day with the watch in my pocket, found the seller, and by referring to his books discovered the number of the watch sold to Anderson, which, I was electrified to find, was identical with that on the gold lever I carried. The name of the maker and description of the watch also tallied perfectly; and the dealer emphatically announced himself ready to swear to the identity in any court of justice. My next business was to visit the man who had cleaned the watch for Anderson in Edinburgh. I was less hopeful of him, and hence had left him to the last, and therefore was not disappointed to find that he had no record of the number or maker's name. On examining the watch through his working glass, however, he declared that he recognised it perfectly as that which he had cleaned for Anderson by one of the screws, which had half of its head broken off, and thus had caused him more trouble than usual in fitting up the watch after cleaning.

"I would have put a new one in rather than bother with it," he said, "but I had not one beside me that would fit it, and as I was pressed for time, I made the old one do. It was my own doing, too, for I broke the top in taking the watch down."

I was now convinced, almost against my will, that the watch was really that taken from Anderson; my next step was to test Burge's statement as to how it came into his possession. If that broke down, his fate was sealed.

When I again appeared before Burge he was eager to learn what had transpired, and appeared unable to understand why he should still be detained; all which I now set down as accomplished hypocrisy. It seemed to me that he had lied from the first, and I was almost angry with myself for having given so much weight to his innocent looks and apparent surprise.

Cutting short his questions with no very amiable answers, I asked the name and address of the man from whom he alleged he had bought the watch. Then he looked grave, and admitted that the man, whose name was Chisholm, might be difficult to find, as he was a kind of "orra" hand, oftener out of work than not. I received the information in silence, and went on the hunt for Chisholm, whom I had no difficulty whatever in finding at the house of a married daughter with whom he lodged. He was at home when I called,—at his dinner or tea,—and stared at me blankly when I was introduced, being probably acquainted with my face, like many more whom I have never spoken to or noticed.

"I have called about a watch that you sold to Burge the tailor, whom you were working with some six months ago," I said quietly.

The man, who had been drinking tea or coffee out of a basin, put down the dish in evident concern, and stared at me more stupidly than before.

"A watch!—what kin' o' a watch?" he huskily exclaimed. "I haena had a watch for mair nor ten years."

"The watch is a gold lever, but he says you sold it to him as a chronometer which had belonged to your uncle, a seaman."

Chisholm's face was now pale to the very point of his nose, but that did not necessarily imply guilt on his part. I have noticed the look far oftener on the faces of witnesses than prisoners.

"What? an uncle! a seaman!" he cried with great energy, turning an amazed look on his daughter. "I havena an uncle leeving—no ane. The man must be mad," and this statement the daughter promptly supported.

"Do you mean to say—can you swear that you never sold him a watch of any kind—which was rusty in the works through lying in a sea-chest?"

"Certainly, sir—certainly, I can swear that. I never had a watch to sell, and I'll tell him that to his face," volubly answered Chisholm, whose brow now was as thick with perspiration as if he had been doing a hard day's work since I entered. "Onybody that kens me can tell ye I've never had a watch, or worn ane, for ten year and mair. I wad be only owre glad if I had."

I questioned him closely and minutely, but he declared most distinctly and emphatically that the whole story of Burge was an invention. I ought to have been satisfied with this declaration— it was voluble and decided, and earnest as any statement could be—but I was not. The man's manner displeased me. It was too noisy and hurried, and his looks of astonishment and innocence were, if anything, too marked. I left the house in a puzzled state.

"What if I should have to deal with two liars?" was my reflection. "How could I pit them against each other?"

Back I trudged to the Office, and saw Burge at once.

"I have seen the man Chisholm and he declares that he not only did not sell you a watch of any kind, but that he has not had one in his possession for upwards of ten years."

Burge paled to a deathly hue, and I saw the cold sweat break out in beads on his temples.

"I was just afraid of that," he huskily whispered, after a horrible pause. "Chisholm's an awful liar, and will say that now to save his own skin. There must have been something wrong about the way he got it. I was a fool to believe his story. I remember now he made me promise not to say that I had bought the watch from him, or how I got it, in case the other relatives should find out that he had taken it."

"Indeed! Then you have no witness whatever to produce as to the purchase?" I cried, after a long whistle.

"None."

"Did you not speak of it to anybody?"

"Not a soul but yourself that I mind of."

"Well, all I can say is that your case looks a bad one," I said at last; as I turned to leave him. "By the by, though, what about the chain? Did you buy that from him too?"

My reason for asking was, that the chain was a neck one, not an albert, and, of course, had not been identified by the widow of Anderson.

"No, I had the chain; I had taken it in payment of an account; but he wanted me to buy a chain, too, now that I remember."

"What kind of a chain? Did you see it?"

"No; I said I did not need it; but I would look at the watch. He wanted a pound for the chain, and eight for the watch. I got it for £5, 10s., and then he went on the spree for a fortnight."

"A whole fortnight? Surely some one will be able to recall that," I quickly interposed, half inclined to believe that Burge was not at least the greater liar of the two. "His daughter will surely remember it?"

"I don't know about that," groaned Burge, in despairing tones. "That man takes so many sprees that it's difficult to mind ane frae anither."

I resolved to try the daughter, nevertheless, and after getting from Burge, as near as he could remember, the date of the bargain, I left him and began to ponder how I could best get an unvarnished tale from this prospective witness. While I pondered, a new link in this most mysterious case was thrown into my hands.

We had been particularly careful after the arrest of Burge to keep the affair secret, but in spite of the precaution, an account of the arrest, altogether garbled and erroneous, appeared in the next day's papers. From this account it appeared that we were confident of Burge's guilt, and were only troubled because we could not discover his accomplices in the crime, and on that account "were not disposed to be communicative," as the penny-a-liner grandly expressed himself. The immediate result of this stupid paragraph, which seemed to book Burge for the gallows.beyond redemption, was a letter from the West, bearing neither name nor address, it is true, but still written with such decision and vigour that I could not but give it some weight in my feeble gropings at the truth. This letter was placed in my hands, though not addressed to me particularly, just as I was wondering how to best question Chisholm's daughter about her father's big spree. The letter was short, and well-written and spelled, and began by saying that Burge, whom we had in custody on suspicion of being concerned in the robbery and murder of Anderson, was perfectly innocent; that the whole of the facts were known to the writer, whose lips were sealed as to who the criminal really was, and who only wrote that he might save an innocent man from a shameful death. The post-mark on the letter was that of a considerable town on the Clyde, or my thoughts would inevitably have reverted to Chisholm as the author or prompter. With the suspicion of this man had come at last an idea that he was in some way mixed up in the crime; yet he did not look either strong enough or courageous enough to be the murderer. Quite uncertain how to act, I left the Office, and wandered down in the direction of Chisholm's home. It was quite dark, I remember, and I was ascending the narrow stair in hope that Chisholm might by that time be out of the house, when a man stumbled down on me in the dark, cursing me sharply for not calling out that I was there. The man was Chisholm, as I knew at once by the tone of the voice, and how I did not let him pass on, and make my inquiries at the daughter, is more than I can tell to this day. I merely allowed him to reach the bottom of the stair, and then turned and followed him. At the bottom I watched his figure slowly descending the close towards the Back Canongate till he reached the bottom, when he paused and peered cautiously forth before venturing out. The stealthy walk and that cunning look forth I believe decided me, coupled with the decided change in the tone in which he cursed me in the dark from the smooth and oily manner in which he had answered my questions during the day. I would follow him, though wherefore or why I did not trouble to ask. About hallway down the South Back Canongate, where the Public Washing House now stands, there was at that time an open drain which ran with a strong current in the direction of the Queen's Park. As it left the green for the Park, this drain emptied itself down an iron-barred opening in the ground, and made a sudden dip downwards of twenty or thirty feet on smooth flag-stones, which carried the water away into the darkness with a tremendous rush and noise. So steep was the gradient at this covered part of the drain, and so smooth the bottom, that miserable cats and dogs, doomed to die, had merely to be put within the grating, when down they shot, and were seen or heard no more.

I followed Chisholm as far as this green, which he entered, and then wondered what his object could be. That it was not quite a lawful one I could guess from the fact that he so often paused and looked about him that I had the greatest difficulty in keeping him in sight without myself being seen. At length he came to the opening in the wall where the open drain ceased and dipped into the iron bars with a roar audible even to me; and then with another furtive look around, and before I had the slightest idea of what he was intending to do, he put his hand in his pocket, drew something forth, and threw it sharply into the roaring, scurrying water. A moment more and my hand was on his arm. He started round with a scared cry, and recognised and named me.

"What's that you threw down the drain?" I sternly demanded, without giving him time to recover, and tightening my grip on his arm.

"Oh, naething, naething, sir—only an auld pipe that's nae mair use," he confusedly stammered.

"A pipe!" I scornfully echoed. "Man, what do you think my head's made of? You didn't come so far to throw away a pipe. Were you afraid that, like some of the cats the ladies put down there, it would escape and come back again?"

He tried to grin, cringingly, but the effect was ghastly in the extreme.

"No, no, Maister M'Govan; I was just walking this way ony way, and thought I wad get rid o' my auld pipe."

"More like, it was a gold albert," I sharply said, getting out the handcuffs. "If I had only guessed what you were after I might have been nearer, and prevented the extravagance. You're unlike every one else in the world, throwing away good gold while others are breaking their hearts to get it. Come; now, try your hand in these; and then I'll have to see if the burn will give up your offering."

He was utterly and abjectly silenced, and accepted the bracelets without demur, which led me to believe that my surmise was a hit. The tailor's gold albert, supposing Burge's story to be true, was all that remained unaccounted for, and its possession now was frightfully dangerous. What more natural, then, that Chisholm should take alarm at my visit, and hasten to dispose of it in the most effectual manner within his reach? If he had put it through the melting pot, and I had arrived only in time to see the shapeless nugget tossed out of the crucible, he could not have given me a greater pang; but of course I did not tell him that I expected never to see it again, and I was right, for the chain has never been seen or heard of since. My thoughts on the way to the Office were not pleasant; afterthoughts with an "if" are always tormenting; and mine was "If I had only seized him before he reached the drain, and had him searched." Then he was so secretive and cunning that I had no hope whatever of him committing himself to a confession. In this I made the error of supposing him entirely guilty. I forgot the case of "Cosky" and "The Crab Apple," who were only too glad to save their necks at the expense of their liberty. Chisholm, though cunning as a fox, was a terrible coward, and as we neared the Office he tremblingly said—

"Will I be long, think ye, o' getting oot again?"

I stared at him in surprise, and then, with some impatience, said—

"About three weeks after the trial probably."

"What? how? will three weeks be the sentence?" he stammered in confusion.

"No; but that is the interval generally allowed between sentence and hanging."

"Good God, man! They canna hang me!" he exclaimed, nearly dropping on the street with terror.

"Wait. If I get that chain out of the drain it will hang you as sure as fate," I grimly replied. I was rather pleased at being able to say it, for I was snappish and out of temper.

"But I never killed the tailor; never saw the man," he exclaimed, evidently fearfully in earnest.

"I've nothing to do with that; it all depends on what the jury think," I shortly answered, and then we got to the Office, and he made a rambling statement about being taken up innocently, and was then locked up.

My immediate task was to have the drain explored, but that was all labour thrown away. The rush of water had been too strong, and the chain was gone, buried in mud and slime, or carried away to sea. I soon had abundant evidence that Chisholm had been on the spree for a fortnight about the time stated by Burge, but my intention of weaving a complete web round him was stayed by a message from himself asking to see me that he might tell all he knew of the watch and chain. He did not know that I had failed to get the chain, or he might have risked absolute silence.

"Ye ken, I'm a bit of a fancier of birds," he said, in beginning his story.

"Including watches and chains," I interposed.

"I was oot very early ae Sunday morning, for however late I'm up on a Saturday, I can never sleep on Sunday morning," he continued, with a dutiful grin at my remark. "I gaed doon by the Abbey Hill to the Easter Road, and when I was hauf way to Leith I saw a yellow finch flee oot at a dyke where its nest was, and begin flichering along on the grund to draw me away frae the place. Cunnin' brutes them birds, but I was fly for it, and instead o' following it, and believing it couldna flee, I stoppit and begoud to look for the nest in the dyke. But before I got forrit I had kind o' lost the exact place. I searched aboot, wi' the bird watchin' me geyan feared-like a wee bit off, and at last I found a hole half filled up wi' a loose stane. Oot cam' the stane, and in gaed my haund; but instead o' a nest I fund a gold watch and chain; and that's the God's truth, though I should dee this meenit."

"Did you mention the finding to any one?"

"No me; I didna even tell my daughter, for I kent if it was fund oot I might get thirty days for keeping it up. I had an idea that the watch had been stolen and planted there, or I might have gaen to a pawnshop wi' it. It was kind o' damaged wi' lying in the dyke, so at last I made up a story and sellt it to Maister Burge."

"You are good at making up stories, I think?" I reflectively observed.

"I'm thinkin' there's a pair of us, Maister M'Govan," he readily returned, with a pawky dab at my ribs!

But for his coolness and evident relief at getting the thing off his mind, I should have set down the whole as another fabrication. But when a man begins to smile and joke, it may be taken for granted that he does not think himself in immediate danger of being hanged. His story, however, might have availed him but little had I not chanced to turn up my notes on the case at its earlier stages, and found there the hitherto meaningless words muttered by Daniel O'Doyle. "Starr Road" muttered in sleep might be but a contraction of Easter Road, or be those actual words imperfectly overheard. Then there were the words about something being "hidden safely there", and the whole tallied so closely that I was at last sure that I was on the right track. These additional gleanings made me revert to my anonymous correspondent in the west. It was scarcely likely that I should be able to trace him; but he spoke in his note of the guilty one being a person or persons outside of himself—known to him. This lessened my interest in him personally, but made me think that if I visited the town I might get hold of O'Doyle himself, which would be quite as good, if not better. I accordingly went to the place, in which there is a public prison, and as a first step called on the police superintendent. An examination of the books at length sent me in the direction of the prison, in which a man answering the description, and having O'Doyle for one of his names, had been confined on a nine months' sentence for robbery. I was now in high spirits, and quite sure that in the prisoner I should recognise the O'Doyle I wanted; but on reaching the place I found that a more imperative and inexorable officer had been there before me in shape of death. Immediately on getting the answer I made the inquiry, "Did he make any statement or confession before he died?" This was not easily answered, and before it could be, with satisfaction, a number of the officials had to be questioned, and then I found that O'Doyle had been attended, as is usual, in his last moments' by a Catholic priest.

This gentleman was still in the town, though not stationed in the Prison, and knowing something of the vows of a priest, I despaired at once of extracting anything from him, but became possessed 'of a desire to have a look at his handwriting. Accordingly I sent him a polite note requesting him to send me word when he would be at liberty to see me for a few minutes' conversation. I fully expected to get a written note in reply, however short, but instead I got a message delivered by the servant girl, to the effect that her master was at home, and would see me now. I grinned and bore it, though it is not pleasant to feel eclipsed in cunning by anyone. I went with the girl, and found the priest, a pale, hard-worked looking man, leaning back in his chair exhausted and silent, and certainly looking as if he at least did not eat the bread of idleness. I felt rather small as I introduced myself and ran over the case that had brought me there, he listening to the whole with closed eyes, and a face as immovable as that of a statue. When I had finished there was an awkward pause. I had not exactly asked anything, but it was implied in my sudden pull up, but for a full minute there was no response.

At last he opened his eyes—and very keen, penetrating eyes they were—and, fixing me sternly with his gaze, he said—

"Did you ever come in contact with a Catholic priest before Mr M'Govan?"

"Frequently."

"Did you ever know one to break his vows and reveal the secrets of heaven?"

"Never."

"Do you think one of them would do it if you asked him?

"I think not."

"Do you think he would do it if you threatened him with prison?"

"Scarcely."

"Or with death—say if you had power to tear him limb from limb, or torture every drop of blood from his body?"

"I don't know—I shouldn't like to try."

"Then what do you come to me for?" he sharply continued, with a slight tinge of red in his pale cheeks. "Am I, think you, more unworthy than any other that has yet lived?"

"No, I should hope not," I stammered; "and I did not come expecting you to reveal what was told you in confession——"

"What then—you wish to know if I wrote that letter maybe?"

"Yes."

"And you'll be satisfied that I speak the truth when I answer?"

"Yes."

"And you'll ask no more?"

"I'll ask no more."

"Then I didn't. Bridget, show the gentleman out."

I was so staggered and nonplussed that I was in the street before I had time to ponder his reply. I was convinced then, as I am now, that the priest spoke the literal truth; how then had the letter been written? Certainly not by O'Doyle himself. Was it possible that a third person could have got at the information?

Back I went to the jail, and by rigid questioning discovered that at the time of O'Doyle's death there was one other person, a delicate man of some education, in the hospital, who complained of pains in the head, and of having grown stone deaf since his incarceration. This man had been set at liberty shortly after, and made no secret of having malingered so successfully as to get all the luxuries of the hospital instead of the hard labour of the other prisoners. There was then an excited and prolonged conversation between this man and the priest I had visited; and as they were of the same faith I have little doubt but the father had bound him down in some way to keep secret what he had chanced to overhear of O'Doyle's confession. This at least was my theory, and a peculiar flash of the priest's eyes when I afterwards hinted at the discovery convinced me that I was not far off the truth.

Chisholm, for his bird-nesting experiment, got thirty days' imprisonment, and Burge, after about a month's detention, was discharged.

The Romance of a Real Cremona

○

A GRAND BALL was being given one night in November at the mansion of the Earl of ———, a great castellated place a good bit within a hundred miles of this city. The dancing room was a perfect picture—the floor polished mahogany in mosaic work, the walls panelled in white flowered satin, with gold slips at the edges, and the whole lighted by hundreds of wax candles inserted in brackets and chandeliers of cut crystal, glittering with pendants, while flashing in the head-dresses and on the necks and bosoms of the fair guests were enough diamonds and other precious stones to have bought up the Regalia twice over.

It was in this scene of brightness and grandeur, and strictly exclusive gaiety, that the curious robbery which was to cause me so much trouble and concern took place.

In an assemblage of this kind, one would expect a thief, if he managed to get into the place at all, to turn his attention to the guests and their jewels; but such was not the case, and it was there that the first puzzling element came into the affair.

At one end of the room, partly in a large recess formed by one of the bow windows, and partly in a portion of the room screened off by a rope covered with red cloth, was a raised kind of a dais for the orchestra. This corner was at the end nearest the door, and clustered within the rope, with stands and music complete, was an orchestra of local musicians, under the leadership, for that night only, of a more distinguished player from England. This gentleman, whom I may name Mr Cleffton, had been engaged at some high-class concerts in Edinburgh, and was about to return to England when he was asked as a great favour and at a high fee to play at this distinguished gathering. To play at a dancing party was rather out of this gentleman's line—to accept a high fee was not, so he went—much to his grief as he soon found.

About midnight, when the room was beginning to become uncomfortably warm, the guests filed out grandly to a supper room close by, and shortly after the musicians were similarly entertained in a smaller room, to which they were led through a long range of carpeted lobbies by the butler himself. Most of the players left their instruments on the seat they had occupied or on the music stand or floor—Mr Cleffton alone took the trouble to return his to its case. He was about to shut and lock this for additional security when he chanced to notice that all the others were waiting on him, and said hurriedly to the butler—

"I suppose the violins will be perfectly safe here? No one will meddle them while we're out?"

The butler smiled lightly at his concern, and said emphatically—

"Not a soul will go near them."

So the fiddle case was left open and unlocked, and its owner went away with his companions to regale himself upon cold fowl and tongue and champagne, or whatever wine he fancied most.

Now, when I say that Mr Cleffton fairly worshipped his own instrument, I am, I believe, giving only an ordinary case—all fiddlers, I understand, do that, and, the more wretched the instrument the more devout is their homage. Whether this particular fiddle merited the slavish devotion I cannot say. It was very ugly, and rather dirty-looking; but its owner, besides never tiring of admiring it from every possible point of view, had given £40 for it, and afterwards spent a good many more, as I shall presently show, in trying to establish at law that the fiddle he had bought belonged to him; so I suppose it must have had good qualities of some kind.

When, therefore, the orchestra had finished supper and strolled back under the guidance of one of the servants to the ball-room, Mr Cleffton's first look was towards his fiddle—or rather towards the case in which he had so tenderly deposited it before leaving the room. Then he started, and blinked sharply to make sure that the champagne had not affected his vision. The case was there, as was also a beautifully quilted bag of wadding and green silk in which he was wont to tenderly wrap the fiddle when done playing, and before inserting it in the case; the fiddle bow, too, was there, but the Cremona was gone.

"Hullo! what's this!" exclaimed Mr Cleffton, in his quick, sharp way, and trying to smile in spite of his concern and pitiable pallor. "Which of you has been meddling with my fiddle?"

Nobody had been touching it, as they all hastened to assure him; reminding him at the same time how he had been the last to leave the room; and then, with concerned looks and widely opened eyes, they looked everywhere about the recess for the missing fiddle, narrowly inspecting every one of the instruments left; but it was all in vain—the fiddle had vanished.

"My beautiful *Strad*! my beautiful *Strad*! worth £400!" was all Mr Cleffton could moan out, as, wringing his hands, tearing at the few hairs left in his head, and almost shedding real tears of grief, he trotted feverishly and excitedly round the ball-room, peering into every corner in search of his treasure.

"Perhaps some of the servants may have taken it out to have a scrape while we were at supper," suggested another player, keeping his own instrument tight under his arm so that there might be no danger of a second tragedy. All the other fiddlers echoed the suggestion, and, carrying their instruments under their arms, followed the distracted leader through the lobbies in search of the butler, or any of the servants likely to throw light on the strange disappearance.

The butler was soon found, and brought out from the supper room proper to hear the story of the Cremona; and in amazement and incredulity he followed the players to the ball-room, where, however, he could only stare and count over the instruments left, with the invariable result of finding them one short. Then the servants were questioned closely and searchingly, but not one of them had thought of looking at the fiddles, far less of taking one out of the room to try it, and the end of the investigation found them exactly where they had begun—that is, staring blankly at each other and saying, "Well, that is strange—how on earth could it have gone?"

By and by odd couples of the guests began to drift into the ball-room, and at length Lady —— herself, the amiable hostess, appeared, and was informed in a whisper by the butler of the unexpected difficulty.

"One of the violins taken out of the room? oh, impossible," she incredulously echoed, with a coolness which must have stabbed Mr Cleffton like a sword of ice. "You will find it lying about somewhere when the dancing is over. Could you not play on one of the other violins, Mr Cleffton, and look for your own afterwards?"

Mr Cleffton looked at the honourable lady in pitying and profound contempt for her ignorance, and deep reproach for what to him seemed an indifference absolutely brutal. What! sit down and calmly play on another instrument while his own—to him the best in the world—might be speeding in the hands of the exultant robber to the other end of the world.

This was more than fiddler humanity could endure. High fees and even the countenance of earls were not to be despised, but they were as nothing compared with the loss of his darling instrument, and in a torrent of excited language, such as the lady was seldom favoured with hearing, the bereaved musician told her so. Not another note would he play till he got his own fiddle.

A horrible pause followed, but in the end a compromise was effected, by which all but Mr Cleffton continued to play, while he followed the butler from the room to prosecute his inquiries in the regions below.

A tardily stammered-out word from one of the servants had given them a slight clue to the strange disappearance. During the interval occupied by supper, some of the strange servants being entertained below—that is, the coachmen and footmen of those who had come a distance, and merely put up the horses to wait till the party was over—had proposed that they should take a peep at the glories of the empty ball-room, and, this being readily agreed to, they slipped quietly upstairs under the guidance of one of the servants, and gratified their curiosity.

"But they had been only a moment in the room," the quaking servant added, "and hardly inside the door."

The butler made no reply, but to Mr Cleffton he hopefully remarked—

"I suspect some of the coachmen will have your fiddle down in the kitchen," and to the kitchen they went to find there more than one coachman, but no fiddle, or trace of one. Every one there seated swore that they had not as much as noticed the fiddle, and then they voluntarily underwent a process of searching. Greatcoats were produced and inspected, pockets turned out, and every means tried without success. Then some suggested that they should see if all in waiting were there; they counted off at once, and found that, by comparing the number with that of the plates set for supper in the servants' hall, they were exactly one short. Who was the missing one! No one could tell, till one jolly-faced coachman said—

"Where's the surly chap that sat next to me, and never took off his driving coat all the time?"

"Ay, where was he?" every one echoed, and soon to this was added the question, for the first time asked, "Who was he?"

There was no answer to either question. Nobody had noticed the man particularly, though to the jolly-faced coachman he had gruffly said that his name was "Smith, or Jones, or something," and that he had been "driving some of the folks up stairs."

Every one in this case, down to the servants of the house themselves, had imagined that every body else knew all about the strange man, and so had paid little attention to him and his odd manner.

Smith had done little but smoke and stare, though he had shown great alacrity in going up to see the ball-room; some, indeed, insisted that it had been he who proposed the treat. More, he had gone up with his heavy driving coat on, and some of the servants had a faint recollection of him loitering near the music stands while the rest of the servants walked round the room lo-oking at the decorations.

"That's the man that has stolen my violin," cried Mr Cleffton at this stage of the inquiry. "He would have a big pocket inside his coat,—probably made for the occasion,—and has slipped my Cremona into it when no one was looking or thinking of him. Who does he serve with?"

"Who, indeed?" All echoed the question; but when guest after guest had been enumerated or appealed to by the butler, there came the still more surprising discovery that Smith served no one—came with no one—and was known to no one—had gained admittance, indeed, entirely by the dress he wore, his own cool audacity, and the general flurry in which every one was plunged by the party being held up stairs.

"Get out your horses, and let the villain be pursued," cried Mr Cleffton, more and more distracted, "the whole robbery has been systematically planned and carried out; but the wretch can't be far off, and we may overtake him yet. I will give ten pounds to any of you who help to put it into my hands again."

The incentive was little needed, for a good deal of Cleffton's excitement had communicated itself to those about him. In a few minutes several vehicles were horsed and ready in the stable yard behind, and on one of these Mr Cleffton took his place beside the driver and with a grand lashing of whips and excited whooping they were off down the avenue, at the foot of which they separated to take the different roads running from the spot. Mr Cleffton, from some idea of his own, had chosen that leading to Edinburgh; but, though the night was clear, and the moon and stars out in the sky, not a trace of the fugitive did they come upon between the mansion and the city. Several tramps they did overtake and rouse up and search without ceremony, but as none of these answered the description of the surly Mr Smith, they were allowed to resume their tramping or snoring, while the agonised fiddler entered the city. Of course his first visit was to the Central Police Office, where he made known his loss to the lieutenant on night duty, and then excitedly demanded to see a detective. It was explained to him that detectives require sleep as well as ordinary mortals, and are not usually kept at the office during the night waiting for such exceptional cases, but this produced little impression upon the musician.

"Everything depends on this matter being seen to with promptitude," he said. "Give me the man's address, and I'll go to him myself."

They ought to have given him M'Sweeny's address, considering the hour and the work I had done the day before, but they didn't; they gave him mine; and out to Charles Street he came at half-past four in the morning, and roused me out of bed, sleepy, stupid, and dazed with having got only three hours rest instead of eight, and, without waiting to see if I understood him, at once began to bemoan his loss.

"My lovely Cremona! my beautiful *Strad*! spirited away—stolen from under my very eyes! Good heavens, what am I to do? What is to become of me if you don't trace out the thief?"

"Strad! Strad! Who is she?" I vacantly asked, thinking from the man's tears that he must mean some young and beautiful maiden, violently abducted from her home and friends.

"The best fiddle in the world—at least, the best that I ever tried, and I've tried a few," he moaned, wringing his hands. "I'd rather have had a leg broken, or lost my head, than that Cremona."

I stared at him, only half understanding the speech, and inclined to think that he had lost his head.

"You don't mean to say that it's a—a fiddle you've come to make all this fuss about?" I at last found voice to say.

"A beauty—and the tone of it, three fiddles in one, and as sweet and soft as a flute," he cried, not noticing my rising anger.

"Good heavens, man!" I shouted at last, "you don't mean to tell me that you've come here and roused me out of bed at four in the morning about a miserable fiddle that you've lost? I thought it was something serious."

"And do you not call that serious?" he returned, after favouring me with a pitying look which was meant to kill me, but did not. "It is serious for me. I'll never sleep till I get it."

"I'm sorry for you, but you might at least have let me sleep—till morning."

"Worth £400—refused £200 for it the other day," he continued, quite undisturbed.

"£400!" I echoed. "Is it possible you gave that sum for a fiddle?"

"No, not quite so much, but that's its value," he slowly admitted.

"How much did it cost you?"

"£40," he rather reluctantly answered.

"There's a slight difference between 40 and 400," I ventured to remark.

"A mere nothing," he said, with the greatest gravity stumbling on a joke; "that's common in fiddle buying. You don't always give for an instrument exactly what it's worth."

"Then its value is just the price which you choose to put on it?"

"That's about it;" and then he hastily changed the subject by narrating all the circumstances of the strange robbery much as I have put them down, only taking much longer to go through.

When he had finished I quietly returned to the point at which he had broken off, pretty sure that he had a reason for avoiding it.

"If the fiddle is worth £400, and you got it at a tenth of that price, you must have got a great bargain?" I observed.

"I am coming to that," he answered, with a groan. "A great bargain? Yes, I thought so too at the time, but I've never had peace since I bought it. It has a history, and as that, I am sure, has something to do with the robbery, you may as well hear it now."

"Then there is more to listen to?" I ruefully returned, with something like an echo of his groan, and a wistful thought of the cosy blankets I had left. "Will it take long to tell?"

"Not very long—it must not, for I must have you and some of your comrades out to watch the departure of the Newcastle trains."

I groaned in reality then, and resignedly began to dress.

"Well, go on—I'm listening," I said, with a very bad grace, which, however, he was too grief-stricken to notice.

"Well, I was swindled in buying the violin—regularly diddled," he said, with some exasperation.

"*You* were swindled? I thought it was the other way?" I said, stopping in surprise.

"So did I, but I was mistaken," he answered, with a writhe. "This was how it happened. I was playing at Newcastle last year, when a man named John Mackintosh, who said he had a real Cremona violin, or one that was said to be real, called upon me, and said he wanted my opinion of it. I had nothing to do during the day, so I went to his shop,—a little den down near the New Quay, in which he sold ginger beer, sweets, and newspapers,— and saw at a glance that it was a splendid instrument. It was of no use to him, for he is only a wretched scraper, who would be as happy with a twelve-and-sixpenny German fiddle, so I determined if possible to get him to sell it. He asked what I thought of it, and I said indifferently that it might be a real Cremona and it might not, but it was worth about £10."

"That would be a lie, of course?" I quietly observed.

"Well, in a sense, yes," he stammered, flushing a little. "You know I was speaking professionally."

"Oh, indeed? Professionals always lie, then?"

"No, no—you mistake. I mean that professionals can never afford to give so much as ordinary buyers with lots of money, But the man was deeper than I had expected—he's a Scotchman, you know, and they're always cursed long-headed. He said, 'Ah, but I wadna gie that fiddle for twice £10.' I laughed at him, but at length I said I would buy it from him, and give him the £20. Blast him, then I found he wouldn't sell it at all!"

"And you came away without it?"

"I tried him every way—pointed out how much more useful the money would be than the fiddle to him, but he only said dryly that 'he would think aboot it,' and thus I left him. The next time I was in Newcastle I called upon him again, and saw the violin, but this time Mackintosh was not in the shop, but an uncle of his, who said he could not sell the fiddle without the owner's consent, but hinted that if I made a reasonable offer for it he had no doubt I might make a bargain the next time I came. Well, I did call on my next visit, and saw the uncle, who said that Mackintosh had decided to sell it if I would make the price £40, and I snapped at the offer at once. I asked when I could see Mackintosh, but the uncle only said, 'You can get the fiddle frae me as well as frae him—if ye hae the money wi' ye?' I had the money, and counted it out at once, while he wrote out a receipt, put a stamp on it, and signed it 'John Mackintosh.' Then I got the fiddle, and thought as I bore it off that I was happy for life."

"But you weren't?"

"I wasn't. I had not been home many days when I got a note, vilely written and spelled, from Mackintosh, demanding back his fiddle, and saying hotly that his uncle, the drunken beast, had no right to *lend* the fiddle to me, or even let it out of the shop. I replied sharply that I had bought it, paid £40 for it, and held the receipt; to which he replied that his uncle had left him, and gone no one knew where, but the fiddle was never his uncle's, nor had he power to sell it, and that Mackintosh himself had never fingered a penny of the price, and did not mean to, but insisted on getting back his Cremona. Here was a nice swindle; yet what could I do? I offered him other £20 to let me keep it, but he laughed at the offer, and then brought an action-at-law against me for the return of the fiddle."

"And what was the result?"

"The result as yet is only that I've had to pay away nearly £20 in lawyer's fees; but, as I stick to the fiddle, and would burn it sooner than give it up to him, I suspect that in desperation he has planned this robbery, and now is making his escape to Newcastle with the fiddle in his possession."

"Oho! and that's the end of it," I exclaimed, now seeing the awkwardness of the case he was putting into my hands. "Was it this man Mackintosh who offered you £200 for the fiddle the other day?"

"No, no! That was another person altogether. But what has that got to do with the case in hand?"

"Nothing, perhaps, but we'll see. Who was he?"

"Oh, a curious, half-daft customer, who has a craze for buying fiddles. He lives a mile or two out from this city, but heard me play on mine at one of the concerts, and invited me out to try his and compare them with mine."

"Did he seem very anxious to buy yours?"

"Oh, fairly daft about it—offered me my pick of his selection of fiddles and £200 down for it, but I only laughed at him. He doesn't play at all, so of what earthly use would it be to him? He has been in an asylum, I understand, at one time, and I could believe it, for none but a daft man would give the prices he has given for the fiddles he has. One wretched thing, with no more tone in it than a child's sixpenny toy, cost him £180. He's been beautifully swindled."

"Swindling seems to be rather a prominent feature in fiddle-buying," was my comment; but while I made it I was thinking of something else.

It is a pity that he told me of the Newcastle affair, for from the first I had caught the idea that the offerer of the £200 would be found to have some connection with the theft. The bringing in of another clue completely upset my first instincts, and made me give them less prominence than I should otherwise have done. The description of the surly, sham coachman, too, did not tally in any particular with that of either Mackintosh or his uncle, though, as Cleffton remarked, that did not go for much, as they might have employed another to do the job for them.

There was little time for either thinking or further inquiries, for on consulting the railway time tables I found that trains started by both lines for Newcastle at a few minutes past seven, and as I could not divide myself into two, I would have to rouse M'Sweeny—rather a joyful task—and prime him with details and descriptions, and set him on to watch one station, while I and Mr Cleffton took the other.

As the early train from the Waverley Station did not run farther than Berwick without a break, I thought the Caledonian more likely to be tried, and decided to take that one, while M'Sweeny took the Waverley. There was no boat for Newcastle from Leith till next day, so we were pretty safe in trying only the railway stations.

We got down to the Pleasance, roused M'Sweeny without compunction, and then hurried off to our different posts of observation. I took up my stand close to the booking-office, with Cleffton watching close by, and there we stood till every passenger had been served with tickets, and the train moved out of the station. Not one carried a fiddle, or suspicious bundle, or had any appearance of having one concealed about them, and not one answered the descriptions either of Mackintosh, his uncle, or the sham coachman. Cleffton was manifestly disappointed, and eager to know what I thought.

"Wait till we hear what M'Sweeny has to say," was my reply, and we drove along to the other station to find that my chum had actually made a capture, and lugged him off to the Office, fiddle and all. Cleffton was in high spirits, but swore horribly when he found that the prisoner was only a harmless blind fiddler, with an instrument having more patches and splices than his coat, and worth only half-a-crown. Then I gave my opinion freely—

"I'm afraid we're on the wrong scent."

Cleffton, however, had formed his own theory, and insisted on all the trains for Newcastle being watched that day; and this was done; but without success. Even then he would have held out, but in the course of the day I sent a telegram to a skilful man on the Newcastle staff, asking him to find out if Mackintosh had been out of town, and at night I had an answer giving a decided negative. Not only was he at home, and serving his customers as usual, but he had even spoken confidently of recovering, his valuable Cremona, in a month or two at the most, by the ordinary processes of law.

"Recover it, the cheating scoundrel!" cried Cleffton, when I read him the message, "after me paying him forty pounds for it!"

"Not him—you did not pay him," I quietly corrected.

"A regularly planned swindle!—all made up between them," he hoarsely iterated.

"I have little doubt it was," I thoughtfully replied; "but did it never strike you as curious that a man in his position should possess such a valuable instrument? Did he never tell you how it came into his possession? It is just possible that it was not really his to sell."

"Do you think so?" eagerly cried the excited victim. "By heavens, I would give a ten pound note this minute if you could fasten a crime of any kind on him. That would be revenge! He always declared to me that he bought it in a disjointed state from a broker in Edinburgh here for £3. Perhaps it was stolen."

I said nothing, for either way Cleffton would lose his fiddle, and probably the money he had paid for it. I had no doubt that the false sale had been planned and arranged by Mackintosh; and was quite sure that the man who could do so would not stick at trifles, but it did not therefore follow that he had stolen the fiddle. I gave the whole matter a night's thought, and in the morning wished heartily that the fiddle had been burned to ashes a year before I was born, for I seemed to get deeper into troubles and difficulties the more I studied and investigated.

I now put Cleffton and his theories aside, and began to work the case in my own way. After getting from him the address of the gentleman who had offered him £200 for the Cremona, I made my way out to the mansion which had been the scene of the robbery. I then worked my way in towards the city, and, after two days' hard work, at length discovered two persons who had seen a man answering the description of the sham coachman at an early hour on the morning of the robbery. One had seen him on the road, another had seen him in the city; but neither seemed to have any suspicion that under the big coachman's coat there was concealed a bulky thing like a fiddle.

From some of the servants I had learned that the man was red-haired and big boned—that he had a slight cast in the eye, and that he undoubtedly knew something about horses and driving. I therefore decided that if I should have the good fortune to discover him' I would find him to be some dodging groom or stableman of doubtful reputation rather than one of my own family of recognised "bairns."

My next step was naturally a visit to the eccentric connoisseur, whom I shall call Mr Turner. It happened, however, that before I had advanced to this stage Mr Cleffton had to leave the city for England to fulfil several important engagements, and I was for a little rather puzzled as to how I should be able to identify his violin, if I were lucky enough to get my eyes on it. Fiddles, of course, are all alike to me, and unless by some marked difference in the colour I could not tell one from another. Mr Cleffton tried to prime me a little by speaking of certain marks and printed tickets which I would find about the fiddle, but when he admitted that some of the fiddles already in Mr Turner's possession had these very tickets and marks I was more helpless than ever. At last a happy thought struck him just as he was leaving town, and he dropped me a note directing me to an old Edinburgh musician who had been playing second fiddle with him on the night of the ball. This gentleman had seen and closely examined the Cremona more than once, and, having a perfect knowledge of all the peculiarities of such valuable instruments, would know the missing one, I was assured, among dozens. To this gentleman, therefore, I went, and we arranged that he should take me out to Mr Turner's as a friend wishing to see the rare collection of old violins. We then set out for the nearest cab-stand, as the place was three miles out of town, and on the way I chanced to say—

"But are you perfectly sure that you would know this fiddle so as to be able to swear to it? It would be very awkward for us all if we made a false accusation."

"I'll know it when I see it," was the confident reply, "and I'll tell you why. I have a strong suspicion that I've seen the fiddle before—ay, and played on it, too. If it's not the £50 Cremona that my old chum, M——, of the Theatre Royal, lost about ten years ago, it must be its twin brother."

"Lost? How could a fiddle be lost?" I faintly returned, as with a sinking heart I anticipated fresh complications.

"Well, or stolen—it was never rightly known how it happened," promptly returned my companion. "I was there at the time my-self; and I'll tell you all about it as we go out."

I groaned, and resigned myself to listen.

We got to the cab-stand, and were soon rattling out from Edin-burgh, and when out on the smooth country road my new assist-ant very eagerly threw off the following information:—

"We were playing at a ball out by Penicuick—six or seven of us altogether—and as it was a jolly affair at a gentleman's seat, we were driven out and in an open trap. My chum, M——, of the Theatre Royal,—he's dead now, as you know,—was leader, and had his best fiddle with him—a splendid *Stradivarius* Cremona, which cost him £50. I had a great liking for the instrument, and used often to try it, and have got the loan of it often when I had a solo to play. We were through with our business about three in the morning, and I remember perfectly that it was a clear, cold night, with plenty of moonlight. We had had some refreshments during the night, but every one of us knew perfectly well what he was about. M—— was the last to step into the vehicle that was to bring us in, and he came out with his fiddle and case in his hand, and said, 'Mind yer feet or I pit in my fiddle—better that you sud be crampit for room than that my fiddle sud come to ony herm.' We made room—the fiddle case was shoved in on the floor of the vehicle among others there lying, the door at the back was shut, and we drove on singing, laughing, and joking, and as jovial and happy as kings. There was a toll-bar some distance in, and I remember some of us getting out to knock up the toll-keeper and get him to open the gate; and it is possible that the door of the trap may not have been shut immediately on the journey being resumed, but, at all events, the door was found open when we came to the next toll, which was near Edinburgh. When we got to the Theatre Royal—the most central place for us all—we got out, and M——, who was joking and laughing till we had all got out our instruments, began groping about under the seats, and then said, 'Some o' ye hae taen my fiddle.' We counted over, and searched everywhere, but the Cremona and case were gone."

"Lost on the road, I suppose?"

"Yes, or stolen—it was never found out which. The loss was not thought serious at first, for there was a brass plate on the case bearing the owner's name, and it was expected that the fiddle would be picked up by some of the early carters coming in to the market, and that a mere advertisement and small reward would ensure its restoration. But though the advertising was tried, and every inquiry was made, the fiddle has never been heard of since."

"And did you not tell Cleffton all this when you saw the fiddle in his possession?"

"No; I was not sure that it *was* the fiddle. But I thought of it, and was very near saying it."

I made no further comments on the new information. I was not anxious that he should prove correct in his surmise, but hoped that the case would be narrowed rather than broadened. With this end in view I thought proper to prime my companion well as to the questions he was to ask the gentleman we were on our way to see, leaving to myself rather the task of watching and analysing.

Mr Turner had a craze for buying fiddles which he never did, and never could, play upon, and I mentally placed him in the same position as a bibliomaniac, who would sell his soul to get hold of some old musty volume not worth reading, simply because it happened to be the only copy in existence. Such a man, I had no hesitation in deciding, would steal as readily as a man drunk with opium. My only difficulty was how to make sure that the fiddle had been stolen at his instigation, and, if that were made clear, how to get at the stolen article.

The cab stopped at a little hamlet about 'three miles from the city, and I was shown into the drawing-room of Mr Turner's house, in which we were speedily joined by a dirty-looking man, very shabbily and raggedly attired, and evidently straight from digging in the garden, whom I had difficulty in believing to be the wealthy gentleman I had come to see.

The face was rather repulsive, on the whole, until my companion spoke of his rare fiddles, when it became animated and bright with the ruling passion of his life. Then he turned to a cabinet in the room, and unlocked it as solemnly as if it had been an iron safe full of diamonds and gold, and brought out several old fiddles, very much cracked and mended, and every one, if possible, uglier than another, and which were placed successively in my hands, with a triumphant look, which evidently meant, "Admire that, or be for ever condemned as ignorant and stupid."

I examined them closely as I had been instructed by Mr Cleffton, and even brightened a little when I found one which had the printed ticket inside of which he had spoken, but on referring the matter to my companion, he only smiled and said—

"Oh, that's a *Strad* too, but it's only a copy, and a very poor one. The other was a *real* Cremona. By the by, Mr Turner," he abruptly added aloud, in response to a signal from me, and while I pretended to bend over the fiddle in my hand in wrapt devotion and admiration, "Do you remember that *Stradivarius* which Cleffton refused to sell you?"

"Yes; what of it?" The words were somewhat hastily thrown out, and I fancied I noticed a kind of nervous flutter in his voice as he spoke.

"It has been stolen."

"Stolen? Impossible!"

These were his words, and natural enough under the circumstances, but it is impossible to convey in print the whole effect of the exclamation. There is more in the manner in which words are spoken than in the words themselves. The appear-ance of surprise and incredulity was—or appeared to me to be—manifestly forced; the eyes of the man had an absent and un-easy expression, as if, while he was mechanically pronouncing the words; he was saying to himself—"Is there any danger? Can any one have hinted to him that I might have been the thief?"

"It is not only possible, but a fact," pursued my companion.

"And how was it done?" asked Mr Turner, with more coolness.

The fiddler briefly ran over the incidents of the theft, but when he came to explain that all the suspicion rested on the sham coachman, Mr Turner dissented warmly. "They'll find that that .has been a cock and bull story of the servants to screen them-selves," he said decidedly. "The whole thing is absurd; and my opinion is that the fiddle is safely hidden somewhere about the house in which it was missed."

"The police don't seem to think so," I quietly observed. "The police!" he scornfully echoed, "a parcel of block-heads—they'll never lay hands on it, I'll swear. When anything is stolen, of course, they have to make a show of activity, but it's all humbug. They never recover the stolen thing."

"I think you're mistaken," said I, with some truth, as the reader probably is aware.

"They'll never see it," he hotly and positively persisted. "I'll stake twenty pounds on it".

"Perhaps you'll lose," I laughingly returned. "Now, Mr ——, you bear witness that Mr Turner has promised to pay £20 to the—say the Royal Infirmary—if the police get back Mr Cleffton's fiddle."

Mr Turner appeared to think this a very good joke, and laughingly repeated his offer. We had by this time looked over every fiddle in his possessions as he averred, and as I had no search warrant, and no grounds for trying to get one, we had to take leave without any further discovery. But while we were being shown to the door by the shabby and ragged proprietor, I busied myself with inquiries as to the number of servants he employed. The house was a big one, and there was at least half an acre of garden ground attached to it, and I was in hope that he might keep a man, or hire one to help him to keep it in order. In this I was disappointed. He kept but two servants, and never hired a man for his garden, unless when actually forced to it by bad health. He kept neither horse nor machine, and always walked in to Edinburgh when business called him thither, so my sniffing after a horsey manservant went for nothing. I knew, however, that Mr Turner had been perfectly aware of Cleffton's engagement to play at the Earl of ——'s, and was loath to believe that I was on the wrong scent.

I therefore bade the eccentric man rather an absent-minded good-bye, and had moodily settled myself in the cab for a good think, when a sudden thought came to me as we were leaving the hamlet behind. A little further down the road from the house we had visited was a wayside cottage with a few jars of sweets and biscuits and a couple of tobacco pipes stuck prominently in one of the windows, thus intimating that the place was meant for a shop. If any gossip—any news or information was to be collected regarding any one in the place, it was surely to be got in such a house as this, and my hand was on the check string in a moment.

When I got inside the cottage, a clean, tidy woman came bustling through from the back room, wiping her hands on her apron as she came. I was a little at a loss how to begin till I noticed some bottles of lemonade in a case behind the little counter, and asked to be served with two.

Chairs were handed us, and we decanted the lemonade in comfort, talking about the weather and roads as we did so, and then I indifferently turned the conversation to the strange customers that the good woman would be in the habit of noticing on the road.

"I suppose you never notice any men coming to see Mr Turner up the way there—a coarse, red-haired man, for instance, in a big coachman's coat, and having a slight cast in his eyes?"

"Mr Turner's no ane to hae mony folk coming aboot his hoose—he's owre greedy for that," was the answer, "but I think I did see a man like that a day or twa syne—no gaun to Mr Turner's, but coming the other road. He cam' in here and bocht a half-ounce o' tobacco and a pipe."

"Going in towards Edinburgh, you mean?"

"No that either, for he asked the nearest road to the railway station."

"He couldn't be going to Edinburgh, then, for the station is two miles farther on, and he would have been nearly as quick to have walked. Have you any idea if he had been at Mr Turner's?"

"No me; I never clapped een on the man afore."

"Was he carrying anything?—a fiddle case, for instance?"

"No, no—naething but a deal box, tied roond wi' a string. It wasna sae big as a fiddle case. He laid it doon on the counter while he filled his pipe. I think there was a ticket on it—put on wi' iron tacks—and a name on the ticket."

"What name?"

"I never lookit. Maybe it wasna a name. I never like to be impident, and didna look very close."

I questioned her closely on the man's appearance, and found that it tallied very closely with that of the sham coachman. Yet I was anything but hopeful of the result. The description might have suited fifty innocent men who might pass her little shop in the course of a forenoon. Still I resolved to follow the clue a little further, and directed the cabman to turn his horse off at the first bye-road, and make for a railway station two miles further on. It was quite a small place, a branch from the main line, and to my satisfaction I found the booking clerk who had been on duty on the day named by the woman. This lad recollected the red-haired man perfectly, but when I said, "Where did he book for?" he looked at me with a puzzled expression, then thought a moment, and said—

"*Did* he book for any place?"

It was now my turn to look puzzled.

"I don't know—I suppose he did when he walked two miles to get to the station," I said at last. "Why else would he come here?"

"He brought a parcel," said the lad, turning to one of his ledgers and flapping over the leaves. "He booked *it*, I know, but I don't think he took out a ticket or waited for the train."

"What kind of a parcel?"

"A light box. I think he said it was to be kept dry, as there were artificial flowers and ribbons in it. Ah, here is the entry—it is not paid you see—he said we'd take greater care of it if it wasn't prepaid—"Sent by James Paterson, to Robert Marshall, Linlithgow. To lie at station till called for.""

"Was the box big enough to have held a fiddle?"

"About that size, sir. I don't think it would have held the fiddlestick too. The fiddlestick is longer, and would take more room."

"Was the box called for at the other end, do you know?" I asked, beginning to be more hopeful.

"I don't know about that—it was sent away, and that's all we have to do with it. These parcels are generally expected, and don't lie long unclaimed."

"You've got a telegraph handy—would you just send a message through, particularly asking if that box has been called for?" and I calmly sat down and motioned the clerk to his place at the instrument; and in a short time had the welcome news that the "box was there still, and had not been asked for."

I looked at my watch and then consulted a timetable, and found that if I drove smartly into Edinburgh I could easily get a fast train to Linlithgow, without waiting for the slow connection with this out-of-the-way branch line. Afraid of looking foolish if I found myself mistaken, I dropped my companion at Edinburgh and took train for Linlithgow alone. The moment I got out, and the bustle of the train's arrival and departure was over, I got the booking-clerk to turn out his parcel press, and easily found the box I was in search of. It was but roughly put together, and appeared to have been made out of the undressed spars of an old orange box; but by shaking it sharply I soon ascertained that it contained something harder than either flowers or ribbons. After a consultation, I was allowed to use a chisel to the lid, and easily prised it up sufficiently to pull out the paper and straw with which it was padded, and found snugly reposing underneath, a fiddle which in every respect answered the description of that stolen from Mr Cleffton.

I had little doubt that I had fairly recovered the stolen property, but I was just as anxious to get hold of the thief. It appeared to me that the sending of the fiddle by rail to this quiet station was merely the adoption of a safe hiding-place till the hue and cry of the robbery were over, and that as soon as the actual instigator felt safe he would appear to claim the box. I could not afford to wait so long; so I got permission to fasten up the box and leave it, while I returned to Edinburgh bearing the fiddle.

My first visit was to the gentleman who had introduced me to Mr Turner, and he identified the fiddle at a glance as Cleffton's; but he did more. Getting out a fiddle bow, he ran his fingers over the strings in a testing way, and at last said decidedly—

"I could stake my life on it that that's M——'s £50 Cremona that was stolen as I told you. Suppose we go along to his house and see?"

"I thought you said he was dead?"

"So he is; but his widow is alive, and may know the fiddle. We will not prompt her in any way, but just show it her and see if she has any suspicion of the truth."

I was so pleased at the identification of the fiddle as that stolen from Cleffton—which was all I had been employed to find—that I offered no objection, and we walked through a street or two to a semi-genteel place, where I was introduced to the widow of the musician, and found her a shrewd and superior woman—one picked out of a hundred, I should say, for quick intelligence.

My companion opened the conversation by asking to see one of her late husband's instruments to compare it with that we had with us, and in the course of the testing he managed that our fiddle should find its way into the widow's hands. In a moment or two I saw her start and look at it more closely, then take it nearer the light and examine it closely at the scroll work close to the screwing pegs, and then she turned to my companion perfectly amazed, and said—

"Do you know what I've discovered?"

"What?"

"This is my fiddle—the one that was stolen from M——, the £50 Cremona lost on the Penicuick road."

"Impossible!—that one was bought in Newcastle."

"That's nothing. I don't care though it had been bought in Australia—it's his fiddle. Look here"—and she pointed to some scratching on the varnish in among the scroll carving—"what do you call that?"

We both looked very closely, and I said at last—

"It's like the letter M scratched with a pin."

"It is just that, and was scratched with a pin in this very room. He did it one night before me, saying, 'If ever any one runs away with my fiddle I'll know it by that, whether they change the ticket or not.' You need not take the fiddle away with you, for I claim it as mine."

Here was a poser, but I was not to be so easily deprived of what was mine only on trust. I quietly took the instrument into my hands, saying—

"At present, Mrs M, the fiddle is in the hands of the police, and as soon as you make good your claim to it I have no doubt it will be surrendered to you, but it seems to me that you will require to advance better evidence than that of a mere scratched letter."

"I for one can swear to the instrument," observed my companion.

"And half a dozen more, when they see it," added the widow warmly. "I will raise an action for its recovery tomorrow."

"Tuts! do not be so hasty—save your money in the meantime," I advised. "I may get the evidence for you quite easily, if I can get the thief to confess. But that will necessitate a journey to Newcastle, so it can hardly be done in a day."

I said this pretty confident that the swindling Mackintosh who had sold the fiddle to Cleffton would turn out to be the original thief, and took away the instrument and made preparations to secure him. I had before this made an arrangement whereby any one calling for the box at Linlithgow station should be detained and arrested; and the whole case now presented the curious spectacle of two robberies, two claimants, and two thieves. A telegram to England, according to arrangement, brought Mr Cleffton down in joy and ecstacy to claim his beloved fiddle, but only to be all but heart-broken with the intelligence that it was believed to be stolen property, and could not be given up till all claims had been fully investigated. The day after, I managed to run down to Newcastle. I easily found the little shop of Mackintosh, and considerably startled him by saying—

"My name is M'Govan, and I have come from Edinburgh about that affair of the Cremona. I want you to come with me"

The name appeared to be known to him, for he became ashy white before I had done speaking, and then with chattering teeth managed to say—

"I can't leave my business; but I'm willing to lose the money. I'll pay Cleffton back the £40 out of my own pocket, if he gives me back the fiddle."

"Out of your own pocket?" I growled. "Man, don't try that on me. The whole thing was a regular plant. But, as it happens, it's not that part of the business that has brought me here. It's the way you got the fiddle—it was stolen."

"Stolen? Then it wasn't by me," he cried, with fearful earnestness. "I can swear that with my hand on the Bible. I bought it from a broker in the Cowgate, in Edinburgh."

"That's a common story—you'll have a receipt, I suppose?" I answered, with a grin.

"I have, and I'll show it you," and much to my surprise he very quickly produced a badly written and spelled receipt for £3, bearing a stamp, and signed "Patrick Finnigan."

"Now, be cautious what you say," I returned, after a long look at the paper. "I happen to know Finnigan, and know him to be an honest man. You declare that you bought the fiddle from him—the fiddle which Cleffton bought from you for £40?"

"I declare that solemnly."

"Then how did he get it?"

"I don't know; but it runs in my head that he said he bought it at a country auction sale. It was in two pieces when I got it—the neck was away from the body."

All this seemed probable enough, but I thought proper to take Mackintosh with me to the Newcastle Central, and have him locked up, while I returned to investigate his statements. Taking the fiddle and receipt with me, I called on Finnigan and asked him to try and recall the circumstances of the sale. That he managed to do when, prompted by several statements of Mackintosh to me—particularly one as to the fiddle being in a broken state, and having hung in the back shop in a green bag, when Mackintosh asked to see it. Questioned then as to how it came into his possession, he said—

"I was out in the country at an auction sale—it was at a farm about six miles from here—and there were two or three fiddles put up. This was the last, and as it was broke—though the auctioneer declared that it only needed a little glue and new strings to make it play beautiful—nobody would bid for it, and I got it for five shillings. I always meant to sort it up, but was afraid I mightn't do it right. One day the man who bought it came in and looked at a fiddle I had in the window, and then asked if I had any more. I showed him that, and saw him look pleased and eager like, so when he asked the price of it I thought I'd drop on him, and said £5. He prigged me down to £3, and then took it away, saying he didn't think it dear."

"You can't remember the name of the farm, I suppose?" I wearily remarked, beginning to despair of getting to the bottom of the strange complication.

"I don't know the name of the -farm, but I think the name of the farmer who had died, and who had owned the fiddle, was Gow, or something like that. I could take you to the place though, and maybe that would do as well."

I thought the proposal a good one, and got a cab the same afternoon, and drove out towards Penicuick, then by some cross roads, through which the cabman was unerringly directed by Finnigan, we reached the farm in question. Here I was not surprised to learn that nothing was known of the Gows who had formerly occupied the farm. Gow himself was dead, and his surviving relations gone, none knew whither; but, in the course of my inquiries, I came across an old man—a ploughman or farm worker, who had served with Gow for many years, and to him I turned as a kind of forlorn hope, though, as it happened, I could not have hit upon a better if I had hunted for years.

"It's about an old fiddle that was sold at the roup when the old man died," I explained, in rather a loud key, for the old man was a little deaf. "It was broken at the time, and was sold for five shillings."

"I mind o't perfectly," said the old man. "It was the fiddle that we fund on the road gaun to market. The maister was on ae cairt and me on the tither; and it was quite dark at the time, but there was a heavy rime on the grund, and the fiddle was in a black case, and I noticed it as we drave by, and stoppit my cairt to pick it up. The maister stoppit his too, and then when he had lookit at the fiddle, and tried hoo the strings soonded, he said, 'Them 'at finds keeps, Sandy. I'll gi'e ye five shillings to yoursel', an we'll say naething aboot this to naebody.' So we shoved it in alow the strae, and there it lay till we got back frae Em'bro'. The maister played on it, and likit it better nor his ain; but on the Saturday after he cam' to my hoose late at nicht, wi' the case and fiddle in his hand, and said, kind o' excited like, 'Sandy, in case onybody should ask after this fiddle I think we'd better pit it ooten sicht for a wee. Get your shuill, and dig a hole ony place where it's no likely to be disturbed."

"And you did it?"

"Deed did I. I dug a hole, and the fiddle and case lay there for mair nor a year. But it was never claimed, and we got it oot, and he played on it for a while, but the damp ground had spoiled it in some way, and he never likit it sae weel as at first. Then it gaed in twa ae day in his hands, and was put awa in a bag till the day o' the sale."

"And what became of the case?" I asked, with great eagerness.

"Ou, the maister used it for a long time to haud ane o' his ain fiddles, and it went wi' it at the sale to Thompson o' the Mains."

"Was there not a brass plate on it bearing a name?"

"A brass plate? I raither think there was a brass plate on it when we fund it, but I never saw it after. Maybe the maister had ta'en it aft?'

"Not unlikely," I dryly observed. "Did you never hear of the fiddle being advertised for?"

"No me; I didna fash muckle wi' papers at that time."

"You must have known that you were as good as stealing the fiddle?—that it must have had an owner?" I sternly pursued.

"I said that at the time, and advised the maister to adverteese it in the papers, but he only laughed, and said he would tak' a' the risk."

"Can this Mr Thompson who bought the case be found now?"

"Naething easier, sir," the man readily returned. "The farm's no a mile off."

I began to see the end of my task now, and, with the old plough-man to lead the way, at once drove to the Mains and was intro-duced to Mr Thompson. The fiddle case was at once produced, and then I smiled as I discovered on the top of the lid a square indentation and two rivet holes, which had evidently at one time contained a brass name-plate. With little difficulty I got the fiddle case away with me, and drove back to Edinburgh, where it was identified by the widow at a glance as that of her husband's lost instrument.

I now had the whole case traced out to its core, and lying clear as a written history before me, but as there was only one fiddle to give away among the claimants, it will be seen that the task before us was not only difficult, but almost certain to bring upon us the dissatisfaction of some of the so-called owners.

While I had been investigating, Mackintosh, thoroughly frightened, had sent a draft for £40 to Cleffton, asking him to return the fiddle at his leisure and say no more about it, but when he was set at liberty he had the doubtful satisfaction of finding that he had lost both the money and the fiddle. I waited patiently to see if the box at Linlithgow would be called for, but evidently the senders had become alarmed, for they never turned up. I then tried to ascertain from Mr Turner's servants if a man like the sham coachman had been seen about that gentleman's house, but they were too wary for me, and denied it point blank. I then turned to Mr Turner himself, and, hinting 'in no measured terms that he was the prime mover in the robbery, *commanded* him to pay over to the Infirmary the sum of £20, which the grasping villain very reluctantly but abjectly consented to do.

There now remained but the two rival owners to deal with, and I am certain the case would have gone to the Court of Session but for a thought which struck me when Cleffton was one day arguing his view of the case to me.

"You gave £40 for the fiddle, and thought it well worth the money," I said. "How much do you really think the fiddle is worth?—I mean privately, between ourselves."

"It would be cheap at £400," he said with a sigh. "I should never have sold it for that."

"Then I'll tell you what to do," was my prompt rejoinder.

"The widow to whom the fiddle undoubtedly belongs never speaks of it as worth more than £50, she has no use for the fiddle herself, and would doubtless be glad of the money. Go to her and offer her £50 for it, and that, according to your own confession, will be £350 below its value."

"Hang it! I never thought of that! I'll try it," he exclaimed, "though I'm afraid even fifty pounds will not buy it, and I don't know how on earth I'm to raise more."

"Perhaps you'll get it for less," I hopefully suggested, but I was mistaken. The value of the fiddle had risen in the widow's estimation, but in a day or two Cleffton came back with a carefully-worded receipt, penned by his own lawyer, and empowering us to hand him the Cremona, which he had bought from the widow for £65. When the fiddle was placed in his hands he fairly hugged it, and kissed it as fervently as I have seen mothers embrace their lost children. I smiled pityingly at the spectacle, but perhaps he would have done the same had he seen the mothers getting back their idols. We are good at pitying each other.

A Servant's Heavy Trunk

◎

"**I** SHOT A MAN last night, have you got his body yet?" said Miser Toddie to me one morning as I was turning into the pend at the Central. I had tried to cut past him, as he was always coming in with complaints, but a sudden hook on to my arm with one of his bony claws pulled me back. His name was really Tod, but the boys shouting after his shabby, gaunt figure on the street called him Miser Toddie, and the name had stuck to him. He was supposed to be a miser of the old school, who kept his boxes of gold in the house instead of lending it out at interest, so several real attempts had been made to break into his house and make the treasure change owners. But for each real attempt Toddie had to tell of several imaginary ones, and was never done pestering us with his trials and troubles. This time, however, he looked so serious and scared that I thought it just possible that he might be speaking the truth.

"You shot a man?" I exclaimed in severe tones. What did you shoot him for?"

"Trying to break into my house to rob and murder me," he answered in justification of his act. "They would get nothing of course, for I'm a poor man, but then they would be sure to turn on me and murder me in their rage, so I must protect myself, especially when the police won't do it."

The concluding words were meant for a stab at me, but much stabbing has made my skin so tough and strong that the blow was never felt. Still a little sceptical, I asked for particulars of the attack, and he gave them rapidly. He lived in an old-fashioned, self-contained house in St. Leonard's Hill, and hitherto all attempts to enter the place had been made on the lower windows. This time, however, the housebreakers had got hold of a ladder from a builder's yard, not far from the house, and boldly broken into the upper flat. Toddie himself slept in that flat, though at the other side of the house, while his servant slept in the kitchen below, and as neither of them were burthened with a heavy supper they were awakened by the raising of the sash, after the pane had been broken and the fastenings undone in the usual manner. Toddie sprang up, and got his loaded pistols, and slipping across the lobby opened the door just as the closed shutters were pierced and a hand came through to undo the bar. The miser carried no light, but he saw the round hole and the hand against the clear sky, and they were good enough mark for him, and without a word of warning he fired. A howl of agony mingled with the shot, and the hand was withdrawn, and the miser left master of the situation.

The scurrying of feet down a ladder had caught Toddie's ear, and he ran down and got his servant to take a pistol, and accompany him to the back green, where they found the ladder much spotted and splashed with blood, but no housebreaker. A panel cutter also splashed with blood lay on the ground close to the foot of the ladder, but the owner had failed to put either his name or initials upon the tool, so it gave no clue. This excellent tool the miser now produced from a bit of paper under his arm, and coolly repeated his inquiry as to whether we had "found the body."

I had believed Toddie to be a cold-blooded wretch, but now I knew it. He seemed to have not a single thought outside himself. He starved his servants and changed them every few weeks, and once actually charged one of them with stealing half a loaf, which I suppose the girl had wolfed up in a fit of hunger.

"We haven't got the body yet, because we haven't looked for it," I replied with some disgust; "but if we do find a body we will know where to look for the murderer."

The miser's skinny jaws and thin lips worked themselves up into a horrible smile.

"Oh, but you can't call me a murderer, nor charge me with murder," he acutely remarked. "I know the law as well as anybody. It was only self-defence. But I've only come here because the man may not be dead, and might come back to try again. If you could get him and shut him up for twenty years I'd feel safer."

I felt inclined to spit on him, but duty is duty, and I had to go out and inspect the house, and see the ladder and the blood splashes, and then go on the hunt for the housebreaker. The ladder was easily traced to its owner, for the name of the builder was on it, and when I got to the yard I found that the thief must have got through a very narrow hole in the paling, from which I concluded that he must have been a small man. The ladder could also have been got through the hole; but it was a heavy one, and I scarcely thought that one small man could have carried it; therefore I concluded that the work had been done by two. I concluded that I had to look for two men, one small in body and one wounded badly with a pistol shot. I went to the infirmary first, and then to the Chalmers' Hospital, but in neither of them had there been any case of the kind. Toddie had expressed a fervent hope that his shot had ended the life of one of those pests of society; but I have here to show that even a house-breaker is not allowed to leave this world, or even retire into penal servitude, while there is any good left for him to accomplish. I did not think that the wounded man could be mortally injured when he had got away so swiftly over an eight foot wall; but I fully expected that he would not have the hardihood to appear in the streets for some time—at least till his wound had healed. It was, therefore, with something like a joyful start of surprise that I met, two days later, a little fellow named Jack Davis, but better known as Dwarfy Dave. Dave was only about four and a half feet high, and small in proportion, but he had more devilment and daring in his small frame than many of my ordinary-sized bairns. He was sauntering past me with a quiet grin in the Lawnmarket when I suddenly stopped, noticing that one of his arms was in a sling. "Hullo, Dwarfy," I cried, grabbing him by the whole arm,

"What's wrong with your arm?" He was always bold as brass, so he answered without winking:—

"Oh, that? hurt it, just."

"Ay? how?"

"Well, I'll tell you," he answered in a burst of confidence. "I got shut into Princes Street Gardens the other night, and in trying to get over the railings I tore my arm on one of the spikes."

"Oh, that was unfortunate," I rejoined in tones as grave as his own. "You might just come down to the Office for a moment and let me look at the wound."

He loudly declared that he was strictly forbidden to take off the rag in which it was wrapped, and that perhaps death or blood-poisoning or some fearful disease would be the result of such an act; but I convinced him that we had a medical inspector who would take upon him all the responsibility of that, and, still finding him reluctant, I handcuffed his wrist to my own and led him thither, he protesting loudly all the way.

When we had the bandages off we found the wound a very ugly one to look at, but not at all dangerous, for the flesh of the arm was simply ripped up from the wrist to the elbow to the depth of about a quarter of an inch. The wound might have been caused by a tear on an iron spike or it might have been done by a pistol bullet. It was the left arm that was injured, and to undo the fastening of the bar on Toddie's window from the outside the left arm must have been used, so theory was in favour of the bullet. But theory is not allowed to convict a man unsupported, and cunning Dwarfy Dave had prepared for everything, for when we detained him he made us write to an apple-woman in Glasgow, who swore most positively that the little imp had spent the night of the housebreaking attempt in her house in Glasgow. So, after a day or two, much to the miser's disgust, Dwarfy was set free. As he left the Central I touched him on the arm and said:—

"You've got off this time. You've tried the miser's house twice now, I believe. Don't try it again, for the third time is not always lucky."

But when did a clever criminal listen to reason? My remark, I believe, only acted with him as a spur to exertion, besides which he had suffered considerable pain and inconvenience through that lucky shot of the miser, and wished to pay him back. Instead, therefore, of quietly leaving the city, Dwarfy went back to his den and consulted with his consort Madge. As in such matters like does not draw to like, Madge was a woman fully six feet high and handsome in proportion, and it had really been she, and not a man, who aided Dwarfy in the attempt on Toddie's house. How she had come to ally herself to such an ugly little wretch as Dave is one of the wonders of the world; but there he was, a handsome big woman with a good face, a smooth tongue, and a fist that could have ended his existence at any moment with one blow.

Where man fails, woman steps in. Adam had not the heart to eat those lovely apples, but Eve briskly showed him how it could be done, and immediately discovered that she needed a seal-skin jacket. Madge derided her husband's efforts, and declared that she could easily take the whole treasure single-handed. Her plan at first was as simple as Eve's with the apples; it was the after-complications that bothered them both. She had some education and easily wrote out a few recommendations as to her character and ability as a domestic servant, quietly waited till Toddie advertised for a servant, and then presented herself as a candidate for the place. Never had the old wretch met with a servant who agreed so readily to his terms and conditions; and he at length engaged her with the conviction that he had by far the best of the bargain. The woman, he reasoned, was big and strong, and would stand a deal of starving before her strength gave way, which would save him several sixpences which would otherwise go in advertising. No registry office would take down his name, as he never paid them, and grumbled into the bargain.

Madge's first plan had been to find out where Toddie kept his sacks of gold, and then simply go into his room some night disguised as a man and choke him into insensibility, and then hand

out the sacks to Dwarfy, but Toddie's stipulations had clearly
shown her that such a plan was impracticable. The miser told
her that he had to protect himself, and that she must sleep in an
attic next the slates, with a single pane of glass fixed in the roof,
and that she must submit to be locked into that every night, and
allow him to lock all the other doors and carry the keys to his
own room. Madge looked at the room and decided that even
Dwarfy could not get through such a small pane, even if it could
be noiselessly removed, and quickly decided that her plans must
be altered. Toddie was a wideawake, cunning man, and he had
the house as well guarded as if it had been in a state of siege, but
it would never do to be baulked, or defeated by a man; so on her
way back to Dwarfy she decided on a much better and more
brilliant scheme, in which that small rascal could take a fair
share of the work and the risk.

"I must have a trunk, you know," she very sensibly remarked
to her husband. "All servants have trunks to hold their things in,
so what's to hinder me to get one big enough to hold you? You're
not big, and it'll be cheery to have you beside me while I'm
working the oracle with the miser. He'll think the more of me
when he sees a heavy, trunk carried in, for then he'll know he
has a hold on me for breakages. Breakages, mind you!" and then
she and Dwarfy laughed themselves sore over the joyful thought
that breakages were to be on Toddie's gaunt body and his chests
of gold, and not on his paltry delf dishes. It is always well to
chuckle over such schemes before the events take place, as if it
be left till after the chuckling may never come off. Dwarfy was
delighted with the scheme, and delighted with his wife for being
able to arrange it so well, and they gleefully went to the nearest
broker's and bought a second-hand trunk, which would have held
a bigger rascal than Dwarfy. As soon as they got the trunk up to
their den they proceeded to arrange air holes and soften its hard
inside with padding of straw, so that neither Dwarfy's newly-
healed arm nor his valuable skull should be damaged in transit.
The same kind consideration prompted them to have the box

carried by two hungry porters all the way to St. Leonard's Hill, instead of having it jolted along on a cab or a barrow. Madge really did take care of her husband so long as it was in her power to do so, and if he was soon led to express a different opinion it only shows that men are born wretches.

When the miser unbolted his door and saw the big heavy trunk he suspected nothing, but when he looked at the two porters he at once decided that they were murderers in disguise, and refused to allow them within the door. It is thus all over the world. Where guilt lies we see nothing, but where there is absolute innocence we discover the most atrocious guilt, and then plume ourselves on our superior penetration.

Madge had to give her new master a helping hand into the house with the trunk herself, and naturally wished to have it carried up to her own little attic. Where should a husband be if not by the side of his wife? But Toddie was blind to reason, and complained of the great weight of the trunk, and insisted on carrying it into his own sitting-room on the first floor.

"It'll be safer here," he remarked, "and I'll make sure that you don't hide anything away in it, for I'll always be beside you when you open it."

In vain Madge protested and reasoned, and declared that she could carry up the trunk herself. Toddie had been bitten before by a servant who disappeared, box and all, in the night-time, and had resolved to protect himself in future. If Madge chose to run away, he would always have her box and its valuable contents.

At length Madge had to yield to a superior will, and leave the trunk in the miser's room while she went upstairs and tremblingly wondered how she should get out of obeying Toddie's command to take out her print dress and begin work. If he was to stand over her every time she opened that trunk how on earth could she get out Dwarfy? Her only hope was that the miser might leave the room for a few moments, when she could swiftly slip in, let out Dwarfy, and hide him upstairs till midnight, when they could begin work together. She therefore took off her cloak and bonnet and ran down and began scrubbing about the kitchen, ever turning an ear in the direction of the sitting-room with an earnest thought of Dwarfy. But though Toddie left the room once or twice he had an awkward habit of always locking the door after him, and the shooting of the bolt went like a death knell to her heart.

"I'll have to strangle the old bloke myself," was her palpitating conclusion. "He doesn't look so very strong, and I am. Besides, if Dwarfy is left long in there he may die through want of air, and if one of them must die it had better be the miser." Once she crept on tip-toe to the sitting-room and tried to get a whispered word with Dwarfy through the locked door, but Toddie appeared to have his ears all over the house, for he rushed down and angrily asked if she wanted to rob him that she stood there at the door of his room. If she wanted anything out of her box he was ready to let her get it, but her place was the kitchen, and she must remain there.

"Wait till night and I'll take it out of you!" was her murderous thought as she scowlingly retreated. Toddie thought best not to leave the room again, and spent the evening there. Most of the time he played draughts with himself, as it would have cost money to entertain an opponent, and when he tired of that he read a religious book on the whole duty of man, for he was of a pious turn, and went to church every Sunday when there was no collection. Ever economical, he saved his ordinary chair from being worn by sitting on Madge's heavy trunk, which he had drawn in front of the fire for the purpose. Now, the air holes had been drilled in the bottom of the box, which was raised an inch or so from the ground by the skirting-board, and as the band did not extend to the back, the draught ran right up on Dwarfy and revived him just as he was almost dropping away into unconsciousness, and drew from him a sigh of relief. The place was still as the grave, and Toddie who had just taken three draught men from himself by a nice corner move, started at the sound and looked round to the door, wondering if he had left it open, or if his new servant had entered without his knowledge. The door was closed and locked on the inside, and he could plainly hear the servant chopping sticks in the kitchen below, so he could only conclude he had been mistaken, and resume his exciting game. Dwarfy had heard the start, and now conceived a splendid plan for getting out of the box. All he needed was to get the miser out of the house for a minute or two, and that, he thought, could not be a difficult task. He therefore in a ghostly whisper uttered the words:—

"Toddie! Miser Toddie!"

This time the miser sprang to his feet, dashing aside the draught-board and scattering the men on every side, while he tremblingly looked round on every side, up at the ceiling, and down at the floor.

"I—I heard something; I'm sure I heard a voice!" he faintly gasped. "It seemed to come from the grave; yet—yet it was in this room. What can it be? Tuts, I'm a fool; I'll read," and he resolutely took up his book and began to read the first page that came to hand, which chanced to he on the duty of supporting poor relations. Something in the miser's conscience twinged at the words, and for the first time in his life he hated the book and threw it from him. Just then Dwarfy whispered in the same awful tone:—

"Miser Toddie! come out! come out of the house and speak to me!"

Toddie sprang up, but immediately dropped down again, his legs refusing to bear him any longer.

G-g-g-oo-ood God! it's a real voice!" he faintly breathed. "Wha-a-at do you want?"

"Come out of the house and speak to me!" returned the whisperer.

"I won't! I can't; I daren't," groaned Toddie. "Who are you! not my sister Jean?"

There was a solemn pause, and then, in a whisper almost inaudible, came the words "Sister Jean."

"I know what you want," said Toddie at last. "You want me to look after your bairns."

But the spirit seemed to want no such thing, and said so.

"You are in danger of sudden death! Leave the house," it whispered, which shows that even a false spirit may sometimes speak the truth; but perhaps the words were less guardedly spoken than before, for the miser sprang up, convinced that his servant must be behind the door playing him a trick. He rushed at the door, unlocked it, and looked out. There was no one there. He ran down to the kitchen and saw Madge on her knees diligently scrubbing the floor. But he had snatched up a cane in the lobby and was too excited to miss the chance of using it, and brought it down in a series of terrific welts on Madge's fleshy shoulders. Quite astounded, Madge sprang to her feet and faced him, thinking he had gone mad.

"What were you whispering at my door for?" he shouted, as she vainly tried to ward off the blows. "How dare you play tricks on me?"

"I never was near your door!" retorted Madge, but then it flashed upon her that now she had a rare chance for attacking and overpowering the gaunt miser, so with a rush she tried to wrest the cane from his hands and get her strong hands about his throat. But Toddie did not prove to be either so weak or so stupid as she had expected. He beat her off easily, and what with the slashing of the cane and an occasional kick and push with foot or arm he at length forced her out into the lobby, where she was glad to unbolt the front door and fly, leaving Dwarfy to his fate. As soon as he had her out he bolted the door and had a careful search through the lower part of the house for any hidden whisperer, but failed to find any. At length he concluded that the whole had been a trick of the servant to frighten him, and was returning comfortably to his seat by the fire when again the weird whisper came—"Miser Toddie! Miser Toddie! leave the house or you will be killed."

The whisperer really meant well to himself, but he spoke in

ignorance of Madge being out of the house, and so unable to release him even if the Miser were absent.

The whisper, however, was enough for Toddie. In an instant he was out of the room, and had pulled on his shabby cap and tottered out of the house, and locked the door.

"I'm either haunted or going mad," was his decision, as he stood there in the cold night air wiping the sweat from his brow. "What's to be done? I know. I'll go up to the Police Office and tell them some one's tormenting me by whispering at the window or door, and get them to come and guard the place till morning. It'll be good company for me, and it'll cost me nothing." He marched straight up to the Central, which he reached just as I was leaving for the night. I hurried past him, but he ran after me and held me fast, in spite of my assurance that there was another man inside far more able to attend to him. "There's some robbers surrounding my house," he said, improving on his first edition. "I've heard them whispering at the window several times, and from what they say I can learn that they mean to break in to-night and murder me, so what will you do?"

"Tuts! you've told us that story a dozen times," I said impatiently; "how long is this to last?

"That's what I want to know!" he retorted with an aggrieved air. "Can't you catch some of them and put a stop to it. It's not imagination this time. I heard them as plain as I hear you."

"Oh dear!" I groaned, "and am I never to get home?" I turned back into the Office, got another man to accompany me, and turned towards St. Leonard's Hill, after vainly suggesting to Toddie that a cab would be a much better means of getting there. While we were thus trudging Southwards, Madge had returned to Toddie's house to make a last attempt to rescue Dwarfy. The windows of the lower flat, being protected with iron bars, were beyond her power; but the door was not bolted within, and was guarded by only a common lock. If Madge had been provided with tools she could have had that door open in two minutes; but unluckily these were all in her trunk with Dwarfy, so she had to fight away with a bit of an umbrella rib and the handle of a spoon which she had picked up in the street. She was at the most critical point and quite absorbed in the task, when we turned the corner and pounced on her. Toddie explained that she was his new servant, but I explained that she was an old acquaintance of mine, and safer in prison than out of it. We hunted all round the house for Dwafy, but failed to find him, and were about to leave when Toddie spoke of the whispering in his room, and we went into that, sighted the trunk, and forced Madge to produce the key. Men, and most of all married men, are the most ungrateful beings in the world. The moment Dwarfy, who had been sighing for liberty, was released by her loving hand, he sprang upon his devoted helpmate and blacked her eyes and kicked her all over with lightning speed; so that before we had him torn off and handcuffed Madge had no inclination to run away, as her eyes were closed up. We left the box with Toddie, who kept it till the day of his death, and led off Dwarfy and Madge, their mutual recriminations giving us ample evidence for the conviction, which put them out of the way for seven years.

Toddie seemed to have got a fright by the attempt, for he did actually hunt out a couple of nieces, whom he had before ignored, and got them to come and enliven his lonely house. But to the end he remained a miser, and parted with money with the greatest reluctance. In his last illness the doctor ordered to him a bottle of brandy to be made into sack. Toddie delayed a whole day, hoping to get well without it, and at last drew his purse out from under his pillow, and opened it with a groan and took out five shillings. "It's a great deal of money to part with," he remarked, and then he sank back and parted with all he had, including his breath.

The Spoilt Photograph

◎

THE PHOTOGRAPHER HAD put up a rickety erection in shape of a tent close to the grand stand at Musselburgh race-course. He was a travelling portrait-taker, and his "saloon" was a portable one, consisting of four sticks for the corners and a bit of thin cotton to sling round them. There was no roof, partly from poverty and partly to let in more light. It was the first day of the races, and masses of people had been coming into the place by every train and available conveyance.

The photographer's name was Peter Turnbull—a tall, lanky fellow, like an overgrown boy who had never got his appetite satisfied. He was clad in the shabbiest of clothes, but talked with the stately dignity of an emperor or a decayed actor. In spite of the gay crowds pressing past outside, business did not come very fast to Turnbull, so, after waiting patiently inside like a spider for flies, he issued from his den and tried to force a little trade with his persuasive tongue.

In front of his tent he had slung up a case of the best photographs he could pick up for money, which were likely to pass for his own, and occasionally some of those bent on pleasure paused to look at the specimens, when Turnbull at once tackled them to give him an order. Women he invariably asked to have their "beautiful" faces taken; men, who are not accustomed to be called beautiful, or to think themselves so, he manipulated in a different fashion. He appealed to them as to whether they hadn't a mother who would like a portrait of them always beside her, or a sweetheart who would value it above a mountain of diamonds. Turnbull's appearance was against him—he looked hungry down to the very toes of his boots—and most of those he addressed were as suspicious of his eloquence as of that of a book canvasser.

At length, however, he did get a man to listen to him—a sailor, evidently, with a jovial, happy look about his face, and plenty of money in his pocket.

"You'll be just off your ship, I suppose, you're looking so fresh and smart," said Turnbull at a venture. "Your sweetheart will be pleased to see you, but she'd be more pleased if you brought her a good portrait to leave with her."

The sailor laughed heartily.

"Sweetheart?" he echoed between his convulsions of merriment "Why, I'm a married man."

"So much the better," returned the photographer, not to be daunted. "She'll want your portrait exactly as you stand—not as you were before this voyage, or when you were courting her. Folks' faces change so soon."

"Maybe they do, but their hearts remain the same," returned the sailor cheerily.

"Well, not always—they change, too, sometimes," said Turnbull, with the air of one who had bitterly experienced the truth of his words; "but with your portrait always beside her, her heart couldn't change. Just step in—I won't keep you a moment, and you can take it with you. You'll have it, and she'll have it, long after the races are forgotten."

The sailor easily yielded, and followed him into the tent, and then Turnbull, having now a professional interest in the man, took notice of his dress and appearance particularly for the first time. The man was low in stature, thick set, and evidently a powerful fellow. He wore an ordinary sailor's suit of dark blue, but had for a neckerchief a red cotton handkerchief loosely rolled together, and so carelessly tied that the ends hung down over his breast.

In order to get all the sailor's face into the portrait, Turnbull with some difficulty persuaded him to remove his cap, and then drew from him an admission that his objection arose from the fact that there was a flesh mark on one side of his forehead which he did not wish to appear in the portrait. The difficulty was got over—as it was with Hannibal—by taking a side-view, and the first attempt came out all right, so far as the portrait was concerned. But the sailor wished to appear as if he had just removed his cap, and with that in his hand, so the first was put aside as spoilt, and another taken, which, though not so successful, pleased the owner better, as in that the cap appeared in his hand. The portrait was finished and framed, and so free and good-natured was the owner that he insisted on paying for the spoilt one, which, however, he refused to take with him. While Turnbull had been putting a frame on the portrait, the sailor took out a long piece of tobacco and a pocket knife and cut himself a liberal quid, at the same time offering a piece to the photographer, which was accepted. The knife with which the tobacco was cut was a strong one with a long, straight blade and a sharp point.

The whole transaction over, they bade each other good-day, and the sailor disappeared among the crowds of spectators and betting men on the course with the avowed intention of enjoying himself, and scattering some money before he went home.

Six or seven hours later a man was found lying in one of the narrow back lanes of the town, so inert, and smelling so strongly of drink, that more than one person had passed him under the impression that he was drunk, and without putting out a hand to help. At length the ghastly hue of his face attracted attention, and it was found that he was lying in a pool of blood, which had flowed from two deep wounds in his breast and side, and thence oozed out at the back of his clothes on the ground below.

Some of the crowd who gathered about him as he was being carried to a house close by identified him as a baker named Colin M'Culloch, belonging to a town some miles off, but who was well known in a wide district from the fact that he went about with a bread van. He was not quite dead when found, but an examination of his wounds soon indicated that life was ebbing away.

One of these was as deep as the doctor's finger could reach, and appeared to have been inflicted with the narrow, straight blade of a long, sharp-pointed knife.

I had been on the race-course for the greater part of the day looking for a man who did not turn up, and heard of the occurrence only when I called at the station before leaving for town. It had been decided that M'Culloch was not fit to be removed, and I went to see him, but found him far beyond speech or explanation. By visiting the spot on which he had been found I discovered a girl who gave me the first clue.

She had been passing along the lane, and had been "feared" as she expressed it, to pass M'Culloch, who was tottering along in the same direction, very drunk and demonstrative, though all alone. Every one was away at the races, and the narrow lane seemed quite deserted, but there appeared in front a sailor, who had no sooner sighted M'Culloch than he began quarrelling with him and threatening him. Thankful of the opportunity, the girl slipped past during the quarrel, having just time to notice that the sailor was a short, thick-set fellow, and that he wore a red cotton handkerchief for a necktie. When she was at a safe distance she chanced to look back, and saw the sailor give M'Culloch "a drive in the breast," and so knock him down. She did not wait to see anything more, but hurried home thinking that it was only an ordinary drunken quarrel.

Questioned by me, she could not say whether the sailor had used a knife. Her idea was that he had only given the man a drive with his hand to knock him down or get him out of the way. The sailor spoke in a low tone; M'Culloch was noisy and defiant. She saw no knife in the sailor's hand, and was sure he was a stranger. She did not think she would know him again, as she did not look at his face, but she knew every one about the town, and was positive that the sailor did not belong to the place. It was the sailor who stopped M'Culloch, whom he seemed to know; and she thought he was quite sober, though pale and angry-looking. "Look me in the face and say it's not true," were the only words she could remember hearing, and they were spoken in a fierce tone by the sailor, just as she was getting beyond earshot.

Having thus a little to work upon, I tried all the exits of the town for some trace of him, without success. He had not gone away by rail or coach, and no one had seen him leave on foot, so far as I could discover; but that was to be expected in the state of the town. Dozens of sailors with red neckties might have come and gone and never been noticed in such a stir. In the town itself I was more successful. To my surprise I found that a man answering the description had visited nearly every public-house in the place. He had never spoken or called for drink; he had merely looked through the houses in a pallid, excited manner, and gone his way.

"He seemed to be looking for some one," a publican said to me, "but he was gone before I could ask him."

I spent a good deal of time in the place, though not sure that if I got that man I should be getting the murderer, and returned to Edinburgh with the last train. I went back again next morning, and found M'Culloch still alive, and sensible enough to be able to give' an assent or dissent when asked a question. But about the murderous attack upon himself he could not or would not give a sign. He would only stare, or shut his eyes, or turn away. The doctor thought he did not understand me—that the patient's head was not yet quite clear; I thought quite the reverse. The same curious circumstance occurred when it was suggested that his deposition should be taken. M'Culloch had no deposition to make, or would not make one. He seemed quite prepared to die and give no sign.

Not an hour later I was favoured with a visit from Turnbull, the travelling photographer. He had been lodging in the town, and of course had heard of the strange crime. He had heard also of my unsuccessful hunt for the sailor, and would probably have gone up to Edinburgh to see me had he not been loth to lose another day at the racecourse; his stance being taken for three days.

I could not conceive what the lank, hungry-looking being could want with me, or why there should be about his lean jaws such a smirk of intense satisfaction, as he gave his name and occupation.

"A murder has been committed—or what is as good as a murder, for the man, I believe, is at his last gasp," he exultingly began. "There will be a hanging match—that is, if you can trace and capture the murderer. Now, Mr M'Govan, you're said to be clever, but you haven't got him yet, and never will unless you get my help."

"Your help?" I echoed in amazement; "why, who are you, and how can you help me?"

"My name you know, and I am not unknown to fame. I am an actor as well as a photographic artist. I have trod the boards with some success, and you know that that in itself is a kind of training in acuteness eminently fitting one for detective work."

I could not see it, and said so. I thought him an escaped lunatic.

"Mark me, Mr M'Govan," he continued, quite unabashed, "I have in my possession the only means whereby you can trace and arrest the murderer. Now just tell me what it is worth, and we may come to a bargain."

"What it is worth?" I said, with a grin. "I don't know that it is worth anything till I try it."

"A hundred pounds? Surely they'll offer that as a reward for such information as shall lead to the capture of the murderer?"

"I don't know that they'll offer a hundred pence" was my reply. "Tell me what you know, and if it is of any use I will see that you are suitably rewarded."

"Ah, that won't suit me," he answered with great decision. "I will leave you to think over my offer; you know where to find me when you have made up your mind."

He was moving off, after making a low and stagey bow, but I got between him and the door, and brought out a pair of hand-cuffs.

"I know where to find you now, which is far more convenient," I quietly remarked. "You have admitted that you know something of the murder—I shall detain you, on suspicion."

"What! arrest me? an innocent man; lock me up in prison!" he exclaimed, in genuine terror. "You cannot—dare not! I know nothing of the murder; I merely think I can put you in the way of tracing the man who did it."

"Do so, then, if you would prove your innocence," I said, rather amused at his terror and dismay. "Were you an accomplice?"

"An accomplice! how can you ask such a question?" he tremblingly answered. "You are taking a mean advantage of me, for I feel sure that my secret is worth a hundred pounds at least. But I will trust to your honour, and put it all before you. People will give you all the credit. Everyone will say 'M'Govan is the man that can do it; we might have known he wouldn't escape when M'Govan was after him.' Nobody will think of me, or hear of me, who have given you the clue. It's the way of the world; one man toils, and ploughs, and sows, and another man reaps the harvest."

"Ah, nothing pleases me so much as envy, flavoured with a little spitefulness," I quietly returned. "It is the most flattering unction you can lay to a man's soul."

"I am not envious," he dolefully replied, "but it is hard to supply another with brains."

"Especially when he has none of his own," I laughingly retorted. "Well, come along; bring on your brains—I'm waiting for them."

"I really believe you are laughing at me in your sleeve," he observed, with a half pathetic look. "It is brave to crush the poor worm under your heel when you know he can't retaliate."

"You're a long worm—six feet at least," I solemnly answered; "a. long-winded one, too, unfortunately. I must leave you in the cells for an hour or two—"

"Oh, no! I will speak; I will tell you it all in half a minute," he wildly answered. "The murderer is said to have been a sailor—

a short, thick-set fellow, wearing a red neckerchief. I photographed such a man in the forenoon, and I have the first portrait, which didn't please him, though it is like as life."

"Ah! let me see it. Have you it with you?" I cried, with sudden interest, and great eagerness.

"Now you change your tune," he reproachfully answered. "I have it with me, or I should not have given in so easily. I was afraid you might have me searched, and, finding the photo, think me an acquaintance or accomplice of the man," and, with a little more wearisome talk, he produced the portrait, and slowly put before me the incidents already recorded.

When he had done I was not greatly elated. The thread which connected his early customer with the man supposed to have attacked M'Culloch was of the slenderest. Then I was disappointed that Turnbull's story looked so real. I had fondly hoped he would stumble and prevaricate enough to allow us to lock him up on suspicion—in other words, that we should find him to be an accomplice, anxious to save himself at the expense of a companion in crime. I took the photograph, but plainly told him that I feared it would be of little use to me.

"Ah, you wish to undervalue it in order to get out of paying me a good round sum when the man is caught," he answered, with a knowing wink. "I haven't knocked about so much without being able to see through that dodge," and away he went, as elated and consequential as if he had really laid the man by the heels.

When I was alone I had a long study over the notes I had taken during the interview. The sailor photographed had stated that his ship only got in the day before, and that he was on his way home, and merely visiting the race-course in passing. He had not said where he lived or at what port he had come in, but the general impression left on Turnbull's mind was that the port was not far off. Leith or Granton seemed to me the likeliest places, and I turned to the shipping lists to have' a look at the names of new arrivals. At Leith only one vessel had come in on that day,

The Shannon; and at Granton, though there were several arrivals, none of them were from long voyages. The sailor had hinted that he had not been home for eighteen months, and that to my mind implied a long voyage; or long voyages.

To Leith accordingly I went, and found *The Shannon*, her cargo already discharged, and only a few of the men on board. Some had been paid off and some were off for a few days on leave. The man whom I questioned—for the captain had gone home too—seemed to me sullen and suspicious. He did not know if one of the men had gone eastwards to see his wife; if any of them lived in that quarter he had never heard of it, and so on. I was dissatisfied with the answers and the man's manner, and had he resembled in the slightest degree the portrait in my pocket I should have arrested him on the spot. I thought I would bring out the photograph as a test. Holding it up before him, I said sharply—"Do you know that man?"

"No, I don't." The answer came out almost before he had time to look at the features. It was too prompt. It was a lie. The falsehood told me more than the truth would have done. It not only convinced me that I was at least on the track of the photographed sailor, but roused in my mind for the first time a strong suspicion that he was the knifer of M'Culloch. I went from the ship to the shipping agents. I found the clerk who had handed their pay to all the men; and on producing the photograph saw that he recognised it instantly.

"Yes, that was one of them," he said, "but he was paid off, and has gone home."

I asked the man's name, and, on referring to the books, he gave it as Tom Fisher. With some difficulty he got me the man's address—which was in a town some miles east—and his trouble arose from the fact that no money had been sent to Fisher's wife for nearly a year.

The sailors' wives often drew one half the men's pay, but she had not applied for it during that time, and was supposed to have changed her address.

"I didn't say anything of it to Fisher," said the clerk in conclusion, "and he seemed quite elated at having so much money
to draw. It's a kittle thing interfering between a man and his wife,
and it might have alarmed him needlessly. If there's anything
wrong he's best to find it out himself."

I left the shipping office, and took the first train for the town
in which Fisher had his home. If he was to be found anywhere, I
thought it would be there—and especially so if he turned out to
be innocent. It is a quiet country place in which everyone knows
his neighbours, and I had no difficulty in finding the house. But it
was occupied by an old woman, who said she had been in it for
nearly a year. I asked for Mrs Fisher, the sailor's wife.

"Oh, she was a bad lot," was the blunt rejoinder. "She sellt a'
her things, bit by bit, and gaed awa' in the end withoot paying her
rent and other debts."

"Where did she go to, do you know?"

"Oh, dear kens. She was a drunken hussy, and thought hersel'
bonny. Some say that she went awa' wi' a baker-man they ca'
M'Culloch, and was aboot Leith for a while, but maybe it's no
true. He used to hae a great wark wi' her."

"And her husband—has he never been here?"

"Never since I cam'; but I heard that M'Culloch was stabbed
at the races by a sailor and I wadna wonder if that sailor turned
oot to be Fisher himsel'."

I thought the old woman the most acute I had met for a while;
we always do when we find a person's thoughts and opinions
tallying with our own. I left the house and pursued my inquiries
elsewhere. I found no one who had seen Fisher near the town, or
in it; but at length there was mentioned to me the name of a man
who had been at the races, and had there seen Fisher and spoken
to him. This man I found out, but he was not nearly so communicative to me as he had been to others. He admitted that he had
seen Fisher and spoken to him, but couldn't remember what they
had talked of. He knew M'Culloch also, and had seen him at the
races, too, but in a drunken condition, and not fit for conversation.

Questioned more closely, he admitted that Fisher was an old friend of his, and that the last thing in the world he would wish for would be to do Fisher any injury by what he should say. He had heard of the stabbing of M'Culloch, and did not wonder at it, the man was so quarrelsome, but he had no idea who had done it. Fisher might have done it, or anybody else—he knew nothing about it, as he was out of the place two hours at least before the attack was made.

I could read the man as plainly as if he had spoken all he knew. There was the same reticence which the sailor had shown on board *The Shannon*, and it probably arose from the same cause—a desire to screen and save a friend. I got back to Leith, and found with some relief that no vessel of importance had left during the two days; I then tried Granton with the same result. "Glasgow" then rose promptly in my mind, and I drove to both the Edinburgh railway stations to make inquiries. At neither had any person resembling the photograph been seen, but a telegram to one of the stations a mile or two from the city elicited the news that a man in sailor's dress had taken a third class ticket thence to Glasgow. He had driven out to that station in a cab, and the cab had come from the direction of Edinburgh. I telegraphed to Glasgow, and followed my message by the first train. When I got to that city I found my work nearly all done for me. Fisher had been traced to an American liner, in which he had shipped under the name of George Fullerton.

Strange fatality! George Fullerton was the name of the man who had seen him at the races, and so clumsily tried to screen him from me. The vessel in which he had shipped was gone—it had sailed the night before—but there was a chance of it stopping at Liverpool. I telegraphed thither and took the night mail, in case the vessel should touch, but the weather had proved too stormy, and she held on her course. Being so far on the way, and now perfectly sure of my man, I did not dream of turning back, but took passage for New York in a fast liner, which would easily have outstripped that in which the fugitive had got the start, but for one or two unforeseen accidents on the way, which added three days to the length of the passage. When we landed, the vessel in which "George Fullerton" had sailed was in the harbour, and my man gone. He was described to me by one of the sailors as depressed and sullen, but singularly free with his money. He had been taken on at the last moment in place of a man who had failed to appear, and so, instead of working his passage, had received full pay. On landing he had treated several of his mates liberally, and had seemed bent on nothing but getting rid of his money.

"I believe I could find him for you; said the man at last, and I readily accepted the offer.

We made our way to a tavern near the harbour much frequented by seamen, and there, sitting alone with some drink before him, I found the counter-part of the spoilt photograph. I should have easily recognised, him in a crowd, but with a fool-hardiness almost incredible, he wore the fatal red neckerchief, which proved to be o silk, not cotton.

I said nothing to my conductor beyond ordering for him a drink at the bar, and then went up and took a seat opposite the red necktie.

"You're a Scotchman, I think?" I said to him at last.

"So are you," he said, a little startled.

"Yes. Long since you left the old country?"

"Long enough," he growled, "and it'll be longer or I go back."

"Nonsense, man," I said, without a smile. "I'm going back by the first ship. Suppose you go back with me?"

"Never!"

The word was accompanied by a deep oath, but I was busy with my hand in my pocket, which came out as he made a gulp at the drink before him, and brought up the barrel of a pistol levelled straight at his eyes.

"Hands up! Tom Fisher," I shouted as he staggered back, and the bystanders came crowding round. "I believe that's the custom of this country, or the right thing to say when two are likely to play at one game. I've come all the way from Edinburgh to arrest you for stabbing Colin M'Culloch. My name is M'Govan, and I've the warrant in my pocket."

He gave in in the most sheepish and stupefied manner imaginable, and some one was obliging enough to snap my handcuffs on his wrists. I took him away in a *coupé*, and had him locked up till I should get the necessary papers filled up for his conveyance across the Atlantic

On the passage home we got quite friendly, and he told me the whole story of the attack. He had met George Fullerton, and been told by him of his wife's faithlessness and flight, coupled with M'Culloch's name. He was quite frenzied, and went off at once to look for M'Culloch, whom Fullerton had seen not long before in the town. He met him at last by chance, and stabbed him twice, meaning to kill him.

When he came to be tried, which was two months later, on account of the state of his victim, he pleaded "Not guilty" by advice, and M'Culloch was called as a witness, when, to the astonishment of all, M'Culloch declared most positively that he could not remember who stabbed him, but that he had a strong impression that the assailant was not the man at the bar.

None looked more astonished than the prisoner, but a moment later he recovered himself and rose to his feet.

"He's telling a lie! I did stab him. I'm guilty, and I'm not sorry. He led away my wife, and she's now on the streets. Ask him if it's not true? That's all I've to say."

M'Culloch, when questioned, made some shuffling answers, and was finally ordered out of the box. Then Fisher, in consideration of the peculiar circumstances of the case, and his having been already two months in prison, was sentenced to a month's imprisonment.

I saw him after his release. He was searching for his wife, and had come to me to get my assistance, but we only found her grave.

The Wrong Umbrella

A GENTLEMAN DROVE up to a Princes Street jeweller's in a carriage or a cab—the jeweller was not sure which, but inclined to think that it was a private carriage—in broad daylight, and at the most fashionable hour. He was rather a pretty-faced young man, of the languid Lord Dundreary type, with long, soft whiskers, which he stroked fondly during the interview with the tradesman, and wore fine clothes of the newest cut with the air of one who was utterly exhausted with the trouble of displaying his own wealth and beauty. He wore patent boots fitting him like a glove, and appeared particularly vain of his neat foot and the valuable rings on his white fingers.

When this distinguished customer had been accommodated with a seat by the jeweller—whom I may name Mr Ward—he managed to produce a card-case, and then dropped a card bearing the name of Samuel Whitmore. The address at the corner at once gave the jeweller a clear idea of the identity of his customer. The Whitmores were a wealthy family, having an estate of considerable size in the West, and had, in addition to the fine house on that estate, a town residence in Edinburgh and another in England. There was a large family of them, but only one son; and that gentleman the jeweller now understood he had the pleasure of seeing before him. He was said to be a fast young man, with no great intellect, but traits of that kind are not so uncommon among the rich as to excite comment among tradesmen. The follies of some are the food of others, and the jeweller was no sooner aware of the identity of his visitor than he mentally decided that he was about

101

to get a good order. He was not disappointed—at least in that particular.

"I want your advice and assistance, Mr Ward, as to the best sort of thing to give—ah—to a young lady—you know—as a present," languidly began the pretty young gentleman. "It must be a real tip-top thing—artistic, pretty, and all that; and you must be willing to take it back if she shouldn't like it—that is, in exchange for something as good or better."

"Hadn't we better send a variety of articles to the young lady, and let her choose for herself?" suggested Mr Ward.

"Oh, hang it, no!—that would never do," said Mr Whitmore, with considerable energy. "She'd stick to the lot, you know; women are never satisfied;" and he gave a peculiar wink to convey the idea he wished to express. "You just be good enough to show me the things, and I'll choose what I think best, and you can send them to the house addressed to me. I'll take them to her myself tomorrow, and if they don't suit, I'll send them back by my valet, or bring them myself."

All this was fair and quite business-like, and Mr Ward hastened to display his most tempting treasures to his customer, who, however, speedily rejected the best of them on account of their high price. At length he chose a lady's small gold lever, ornamented with jewels on the back, and a set of gold earrings, with brooch and necklet to match. The price of the whole came to a trifle under £60, and the buyer expressed much satisfaction at the reasonable charges and the beauty of the articles.

"You will put them up carefully and send them home, and, if I keep them, you can send in your bill at the usual time," said the agreeable customer; and so the pleasant transaction concluded, the jeweller showed him out, the cab was entered, and Mr Whitmore not only disappeared from the jeweller's sight, but also, as it seemed, from every one else's. As he left the shop, the languid gentleman had looked at his watch, and the jeweller had just time to notice that it was an expensive gold one, with a very peculiar dial of gold figures on a black ground. Some reference had also

been made to diamonds during the selection of the presents, and
Mr Whitmore had been obliging enough to remove one of the rings
from his white fingers and place it in the hands of the jeweller,
when that gentleman read inside the initials "S. W."

These two circumstances were afterwards to add to the intri-
cacy of the case when it came into our hands. From the moment
when the pretty-faced gentleman was shown out by Mr Ward, he
could not have vanished more effectually if he had driven out of
the world. Half an hour after, a young apprentice lad in Mr Ward's
employ took the small parcel given him by his master out to the
stately residence of the Whitmores at the West End, and, according to his statement afterwards, duly delivered the same.
There was no nameplate upon the door, but there was a big brass
number which corresponded with that on the card left by the
pleasant customer. The messenger, who was no stupid boy, but a
lad of seventeen, declared most positively that he looked for the
number in that fine crescent, rang the bell, and was answered by
a dignified footman. He then asked if the house was that of the
Whitmores, was answered with a stately affirmative, and then
departed. None of the articles thus sent home were returned,
and they were therefore entered in the books as sold. A month
or two later the account was made up and sent to the buyer.
There was no response for many weeks, but at length the answer
did come, and in a manner altogether unexpected. A gentleman, young, but by no means good-looking, drove up to the
shop door one forenoon and entered the shop. Mr Ward had
never seen him before, but the card which he placed before the
jeweller was familiar enough to cause him to start strangely. It
bore the name, "Samuel Whitmore," with the address at the
lower corner—it was, indeed, the facsimile of that which had
been produced by Mr Ward's languid but agreeable customer
months before.

"I wish to see Mr Ward," said the new comer, evidently as
ignorant of the jeweller's appearance as that gentleman was of
his.

"I am Mr Ward, sir," was the reply; and then the stranger brought out some papers, from which he selected Mr Ward's account for the articles of jewellery, which he placed before the astonished tradesman, with the words—

"I am Mr Whitmore, and this account has been sent to me by mistake. It would have been checked sooner, but it happened that I was away in Paris when it was sent, and as I was expected home they did not trouble to forward the paper."

The jeweller stared at his visitor. He was a young man, and wore Dundreary whiskers, and had on his fingers just such rings as Mr Ward remembered seeing on the hand of his customer, but there was not the slightest resemblance of features.

"You Mr Samuel Whitmore?" he vacantly echoed, picking up the card of the gentleman, and mentally asking himself whether he was dreaming or awake.

"Mr Samuel Whitmore," calmly answered the gentleman.

"Son of Mr Whitmore of Castleton Lee?"

"The same, sir."

"Then you have a brother, I suppose?" stammered the jeweller. "There has been a mistake of some kind."

"I have no brother, and never had," quietly answered his visitor; "and I never bought an article in this shop that I know of; and certainly did not purchase the things which you have here charged against me."

"A gentleman came here—drove up in a cab, just as you have done—and presented a card like this," said the jeweller, beginning to feel slightly alarmed. "Surely I have not been imposed upon? and yet that is impossible, for the things were safely sent home and delivered at your house."

The gentleman smiled, and shook his head.

"I thought it possible that my father might have ordered and received these things," he politely observed, "but on making inquiry I learned that not only was that not the case, but no such articles ever came near the house."

This was too much for the jeweller. He touched a bell and had the apprentice lad, Edward Price, sent for, and drew from him such a minute account of the delivery of the parcel, that it became the gentleman's turn to be staggered and to doubt his own convictions. The lad described the house, the hall, and the clean-shaven footman so clearly and accurately that his narrative bore an unmistakable impress of truthfulness. The gentleman could, therefore, only suggest the possibility of Price having mistaken the number of the house, and the things being accepted as a present by the persons who had thus received them by mistake. But even this supposition—which was afterwards proved to be fallacious—did not account for the most mysterious feature in the case—how the things had been ordered and by whom. It was clear to Mr Ward that the gentleman before him and the buyer of the presents were two distinct persons, having no facial resemblance; but the new Mr Whitmore having, in his impatience to be gone, drawn from his pocket a gold watch, with the peculiar black dial already described, a fresh shade of mystery was cast over the case.

"I have seen that watch before," he ventured to say. "The gentleman who ordered the things wore just such a watch as that. I saw it when he was leaving. And he had on his finger a diamond ring very like that which you wear. I had it in my hand for a few moments, and it bore his initials inside."

The gentleman, looking doubly surprised, drew from his finger the ring in question and placed it in the jeweller's hand. The initials "S. W." were there inside, exactly as he had seen them on the ring of the mysterious representative.

"Did you ever lend this ring to any one?" he asked in amazement.

"Never; and, what is more, it is never off my finger but when I am asleep," was the decided reply; and then he listened patiently while Mr Ward related the whole of the circumstances attending the selection of the articles. No light was thrown on the matter by the narrative; but the gentleman, who before had been somewhat angry and impatient, now sobered down, and showed sufficient interest to advise Mr Ward to put the case in our hands, promising him every assistance in his power to get at the culprit. This advice was acted upon, and the next day I was collecting the facts I have recorded. I had no idea of the lad Price being involved in the affair, but I nevertheless thought proper to make sure of every step by taking him out to the Crescent and getting him to show me the house at which he delivered the parcel. He conducted me without a moment's hesitation to the right house. I rang the bell, and when the door was opened by a clean-shaven footman, Price rapidly identified the various features of the hall. He failed, however, to identify the footman as the person who had taken the parcel from him. I was not disappointed, but rather pleased at that circumstance. I had begun to believe that the footman, like the purchaser, was a "double." Being now on the spot, I asked to see Mr Samuel Whitmore, and, being shown up, I began to question that gentleman as to his whereabouts on the day of the purchase. That was not easily settled. Mr Whitmore's time was his own, and one day was so very like another with him that he frankly told me that to answer that question was quite beyond his power.

By referring to Mr Ward's account, however, we got the exact day and month of the purchase, and the naming of the month quickened the gentleman's memory. That day had been one of many days spent in the same manner, for he had been two weeks confined to bed by illness. He could not give me the exact date, but I guessed rightly that his medical man would have a better idea, and, getting that gentleman's address, I soon found beyond doubt that Mr Samuel Whitmore had on the day of the purchase been confined to his own room, and so ill that his life was in actual danger.

"Some of his friends may have personated him for a lark," was my next thought, but a few inquiries soon dispelled that idea. None of Mr Whitmore's friends had looked near him during his illness, and to complete the impersonation, it was necessary that they should have had his ring and watch, which he declared had never been out of his possession.

The discovery of these facts narrowed down the inquiry considerably. They all seemed to focus towards that invisible and mysterious footman who had taken in the parcel.

There is a great deal in a name. The lad Price had used the word "footman" in describing the servant, probably because he had a vague idea that any one was a footman who wore livery and opened a door. It had never struck him to ask if there was any other man-servant in the house, and it might not have struck me either if I had not seen another—a valet—busy brushing his young master's clothes in a bedroom close to the apartment in which we conversed.

"Who is that brushing the clothes?" I asked of Mr Whitmore. "The coachman?"

"Oh, no; the coachman does not live in the house while we are in town; that's my valet."

"And what does he do?"

"Attends me—gets my clothes, helps me to dress—looks after everything, and serves me generally."

"Does he ever answer the door bell?"

"Really, I could not say," was the answer, somewhat wearily given, "but you may ask him."

The gentleman, I could see, had a sovereign contempt for both me and my calling, and was impatient to see me gone; but that, of course, did not disturb me in the least.

I had the valet called in, and in reply to my question he gave me to understand very clearly that answering the door bell "was not his work," but lay entirely between the footman and tablemaid.

"Supposing they were both out of the way, and you were near the door when the bell rang, would you not answer it by opening the door?"

"No, certainly not."

He appeared to think me very simple to ask such a question.

"Then who would open the door?"

"I don't knew; somebody else—it wouldn't be me; but they

wouldn't be both out of the way at once without leaving some one to attend the door."

"Just so; and that one might be you. Now don't interrupt, and try to carry your mind back five months, and to the 21st day of that month, while your master here lay ill, and tell me if you did not answer the door bell and take in a small parcel addressed to your master?"

"I wasn't here five months ago, sir," was the quick response; "I was serving in the north then."

"Indeed!" and I turned to his master in some surprise; "have you discharged your valet within that time?"

"Oh, yes," he lazily drawled; "I had Atkinson before him."

"At the time you were ill?"

"Possibly so. I really don't remember."

"You did not tell me of this before."

"No? Well, it doesn't matter much, I suppose?"

I found it difficult to keep my temper. I had the lad Price brought up from the hall, and he said most decidedly that the valet before us was not the man who had taken in the parcel.

"Why did Atkinson leave you?" I resumed, to the master.

"He did not leave exactly. I was tired of him. He put on so many airs that some thought that he was the master and I the man—fact, I assure you. He was too fast, and conceited, and vain; and I thought—though I'd be the last to say it—he wasn't quite what you call honest, you know."

"Good-looking fellow?"

"Oh, passable as to that," was the somewhat grudging reply. Mr Whitmore himself was very ugly.

"Did he ever put on your clothes—that is, wear them when you were not using them yourself?"

"Oh, yes; the beggar had impudence enough for anything."

"And your jewellery, and watch, too, I suppose?"

"Well, I don't know as to that—perhaps he did. I could believe him capable of anything that was impudent—coolest rascal I ever met. I tell you, Mr—Mr—Mr M'Fadden—I beg your pardon,

M'Gadden—ah, I'm not good at remembering names—I tell you, I've an idea; just struck me, and you're as welcome to it as if it were your own. P'r'aps that rascal Atkinson has ordered those things, and got them when they were sent home. Rather smart of me to think of that, eh?"

"Very smart," I answered, with great emphasis, while his valet grinned behind a coat. "The affinity of great minds is shown in the fact that the same idea struck me. Can you help me to Atkinson's present address?"

He could. Although he had been wearied and disgusted with the fellow himself, he had not only given Atkinson a written character of a high order, but personally recommended him to one of his acquaintances with whom, he presumed, the man was still serving. I took down the address and left for Moray Place, taking the lad Price with me. When we came to the house a most distinguished-looking individual opened the door—much haughtier and more dignified than a Lord of State—and while he was answering my inquiries, the lad Price gave me a suggestive nudge. When I quickly turned in reply and bent my ear, he whispered—

"That's like the man that took the parcel from me at Whitmore's."

"Like him? Can you swear it is him?"

The lad took another steady look at the haughty flunkey, and finally shook his head and said, "No, I cannot swear to him, but it is like him."

The haughty individual was John Atkinson, formerly valet to Mr Whitmore. A few questions, a second look at the lad Price, and one naming of Mr Ward the jeweller, disturbed his highness greatly, but failed to draw from him anything but the most indignant protestations of innocence.

I decided to risk the matter and take him with me. He insisted upon me first searching his room and turning over all his possessions, to show that none of the articles were in his keeping. I felt certain of his guilt. There was in his manner an absence of that flurry and excitement with which the innocent always greet an accusation of the kind; but his cool request as to searching made me a little doubtful of bringing the charge home to him. It convinced me, at least, that the articles themselves were far beyond our reach. From this I reasoned that they had not been procured for the ordinary purposes of robbery—that is, to be sold or turned into money.

The buyer had said that they were intended as a present for a lady: could it be possible that he had told the truth?

I began to have a deep interest in Atkinson's love affairs and a strong desire to learn who was the favoured lady. On our way to the Office I called in at Mr Ward's, but the jeweller failed to identify Atkinson as the buyer of the articles. He was like him, he said, but the other had Dundreary whiskers, and this man was clean shaven. Afterwards, when I had clapped a pair of artificial whiskers upon Atkinson, the jeweller was inclined to alter his opinion and say positively that it was the man, but, on the whole, the case was so weak that it never went to trial

Atkinson was released, and returned to his place "without a stain upon his character," and so justice appeared to be defeated. The first act of the drama had ended with villainy triumphant.

Let me now bring on "the wrong umbrella." A great party was given, some months after, in a house in the New Town, and, as usual at such gatherings, there was some confusion and accidental misappropriation at the close. All that happened was easily explained and adjusted, but the case of the umbrella. Most of the guests had come in cabs, but one or two living near had come on foot, bringing umbrellas with them. The number of these could have been counted on the fingers of one hand, yet, when the party was over, the lady of the house discovered that a fine gold-mounted ivory-handled umbrella of hers had been taken, and a wretched alpaca left in its place. The missing umbrella was a present, and therefore highly prized; it was also almost fresh from the maker. It was rather suggestive, too, that the wretched thing left in its place was a gentleman's umbrella—a big, clumsy thing, which could not have been mistaken for the other by a blind man It seemed therefore more like a theft than a mistake, and after fruitless inquiries all round, the lady sent word to us, and a full description of the stolen umbrella was entered in the books.

The theory formed by the owner was that the umbrella had been stolen by some thief who had gained admittance during the confusion, and that the umbrella left in its place had simply been forgotten by some of the guests, and had no connection with the removal of her own. Reasoning upon this ground, I first tried the pawnbrokers, without success, and then, remembering that the missing article had been heavily mounted with gold, I thought of trying some of the jewellers to see if they had bought the mounting as old gold. I had no success on that trial either, but, to my astonishment and delight, M'Sweeny, whom I had sent out to hunt on the same lines in the afternoon, brought in the umbrella, safe and sound, as it had been taken from the owner's house. The surprising thing was that the umbrella had been got in a jeweller's shop, at which it had been left by a gentleman to get the initials K. H. engraved on the gold top. It was a mere chance remark which led to its discovery, for when M'Sweeny called the umbrella was away at an engraver's, and had to be sent for.

I went over to the New Town very quickly and showed the umbrella to the lady, who identified it—with the exception of the initials—and showed marks and points about the ivory handle which proved it hers beyond doubt. I kept the umbrella, and went to the jeweller who had undertaken the engraving of the initials. He described the gentleman who had left the umbrella, and, turning up his books, gave me the name and address, which I soon found to be fictitious. He stated, however, that the umbrella was to be called for on the following day, and I arranged to be there at least an hour before the stated time to receive him. When I had been there a couple of hours or so—seated in the back shop reading the papers—a single stroke at a bell near me, connected with the front shop, told me that my man had come. I advanced and looked through a little pane of glass, carefully concealed from the front, and took a good look at him. What was my astonishment to find that the "gentleman" was no other than my old acquaintance, John Atkinson, the valet!

According to the arrangement I had made with the jeweller—in anticipation of finding the thief to be a man in a good position in society—the umbrella was handed over to the caller, the engraving paid for, and the man allowed to leave the shop.

I never followed any one with greater alacrity or a stronger determination not to let him slip. I fully expected him to go to his place in Moray Place, and intended to just let him get comfortably settled there, and then go in and arrest him before his master, who had been very wrathful at the last "insult to his trusted servant."

But John did not turn his face in that direction at all. He moved away out to a quiet street at the South Side, where he stopped before a main door flat bearing the name "Miss Huntley" on a brass plate. A smart servant girl opened the door, and John was admitted by her with much deference.

When he had been in the house a short time, I rang the bell and asked for him.

"He is with Miss Huntley," said the girl, with some embarrassment, evidently wishing me to take the hint and leave.

"Indeed! and she is his sweetheart, I suppose?"

The girl laughed merrily, and said she supposed so.

I only understood that laugh when I saw Miss Huntley—a toothless old woman, old enough to be my mother, or John's grandmother. From the girl I learned that her mistress was possessed of considerable property, and that John and she were soon to be made one.

I doubted that, but did not say so. I had no qualms whatever, and sharply demanded to be shown in. John became ghastly pale the moment he sighted my face. Miss Huntley had the stolen umbrella in her hands, and was admiringly examining her initials on the gold top.

"Is that your umbrella, ma'am?" I asked, in a tone which made her blink at me over her spectacles.

"Yes, I've just got it in a present from Mr Atkinson," she answered.

"Oh, indeed! And did he give you any other presents?" I sternly pursued, as John sank feebly into a chair.

She refused to answer until I should say who I was and what was my business there; but when I did explain matters, the poor old skeleton was quite beyond answering me. She was horrified at the discovery that John was a thief, but more so, I am convinced, to find that he was not a gentleman at all, but only a flunkey. In the confusion of her fainting and hysterics, I had the opportunity of examining the gold watch, which was taken from her pocket by the servant, and found inside the back of the case a watch-paper bearing Mr Ward's name and address, and also the written date of the sale, which corresponded exactly with that already in my possession. The brooch and other articles were readily given up by Miss Huntley, as soon as she was restored to her senses. Had she been fit for removal, we should have taken her too, but the shock had been too much for her, and her medical man positively forbade the arrest.

John made a clean breast of the swindle and impersonation, and went to prison for a year, while the poor old woman he had made love to went to a grave which could scarcely be called early. I met John some years after in a seedy and broken-down condition, and looking the very opposite of the haughty aristocrat he had seemed when first we met. I scarcely recognised him, but when I did, I said significantly—

"Ah, it's you? I'm afraid, John, you took the wrong umbrella that time!"

"I did," he impressively returned, with a rueful shake of the head; and I saw him no more.

Benjie Blunt's Clever Alibi

◉

Ow BENJIE BLUNT came to get his name I never could
discover—possibly it was prompted by the law of
contrariety, because Benjie was so sharp. His real
name had not the remotest resemblance to this, but as he refused to answer to that, he was always put down in the prison
books as Benjamin Blunt.

Benjie's vanity was much greater than his acquisitiveness.
He liked to boast of the feats he had done, hence the cases in
which he was mixed up generally showed a superlative degree
of ingenuity and cunning, however small the stake. I do not find,
however, that Benjie's cleverness produced any marked diminution
in the number of his convictions—indeed, it was the grave length
of that list which prompted him to make such elaborate preparations in the following case.

Close to the Meadows, and before that quarter was so much
built upon, there was a cottage occupied by an old army surgeon, whom I may name Dr Temple, and his servant, Peggy Reid.
This gentleman was a bachelor, and somewhat eccentric, and,
as he had spent the most of his life in India, he was supposed to
be very rich. Dr Temple was as exact and punctual in his habits
and engagements as if he had been still in the army. Everything
went on like clock-work in his snug little home, and if a servant
did not please him in that respect, he discharged her on the spot.
One of his habits was to spend every Thursday evening at a
friend's house, leaving his own house at seven o'clock, and returning at half-past ten. His house was full of Indian curiosities
and nicknacks, but most of them were of a kind which could not

have been readily turned into money. The cottage had a little garden in front, railed in, and had also a space at one end, in which stood a coal cellar, a wash-house, and an empty dog kennel.

A working joiner happened to be passing this cottage about nine o'clock on a Thursday night, and, glancing up towards the front door, was surprised not so much at seeing it standing half-open as at noticing something like a human foot and the skirt of a dress lying motionless on the lobby floor. There was a light in the lobby, and the inner glass door was also ajar. The man stopped and stared, wondering whether it was not some servant busy scrubbing the floor, and lying on her side to reach some corner scarcely accessible. But the foot did not move, and as the place was lonely and dark, the man suspected something was wrong, looked round for a policeman in vain, and then pushed open the gate and advanced towards the strange object. He found Dr Temple's servant, Peggy Reid, lying on the lobby floor behind the outer door quite insensible. At first the man thought she had been knocked down, and so stunned, but seeing no traces of a blow, and finding that she breathed calmly and regularly, he came to the conclusion that she was drunk, and vainly tried to arouse her by shaking her and propping her up on a lobby chair. As she gave but faint signs of awaking, he then tried to call the assistance of the household by ringing the bell, and, getting no response, concluded that the house was empty, and went in search of a policeman. At the Middle Walk he was fortunate enough to catch the glare of a policeman's lantern, and soon had the man informed of the strange discovery. They went back together to the cottage, and found the servant girl still sitting in the lobby, and looking stupid and confused.

"A man rang the bell and said the doctor sent him for his stick," she feebly explained in reply to the policeman's questions. "Then he shoved himself in and held something to my mouth, and everything grew dark."

"Chloroform," said the policeman shortly. "The house has been robbed, I'll swear. Let's look through it and see."

With some assistance Peggy was able to get on her feet and lead them through the house. A great deal of damage had been done; ornaments and curiosities smashed and tossed down in sheer wantonness or anger, but not much of value taken. Some silver ornaments and jewellery, and an old-fashioned gold watch, were all that the servant could say positively were gone; but it turned out afterwards that a considerable sum of money in gold and bank notes had been taken besides these valuables. An Indian casket of carved wood, ornamented with ivory, was also missed on the day following. It was not worth sixpence to any one but the owner, and why it had been taken was a mystery to all.

While this discovery was being made, or possibly a short time before, a curious arrest was being made in the High Street, which, as everyone knows, is about seven minutes' walk from the Meadows. Benjie Blunt had made his appearance in the High Street, not far from the Central Station, uproariously drunk and apparently reckless of all consequences. He staggered about, shouting out sundry sounds which were supposed to represent a song, he insulted everyone within his reach, and, finally, in making a mad grasp at some of the tormenting gamins clustered about him, he fell forward on his face, and was so overcome that he could not get up again. A crowd cannot gather in the High Street at any time without almost instantly attracting our attention. The man on the beat was soon at Benjie's side, and on telling him to get up was rewarded with a kick on the shin bone. Another man had to be summoned, and between them, with the greatest difficulty, they managed to carry the limp and drooping figure of Benjie into the station by which time that worthy was quite incapable of speech, and was locked in a cell to sober at leisure. Benjie passed the night in a profound slumber, and was next morning placed at the bar of the Police Court, and fined five shillings, or seven days. When had a professional thief five shillings to spare? or the inclination to part with the sum, unless he had urgent and profitable work awaiting him outside?

Benjie declared himself bankrupt, and made a pathetic appeal to the Sheriff to be let off "just this once," and was then hustled out and taken to the cells, no more depressed than if he had been starting for a week's holidays. Indeed, from the manner in which he thrust his tongue into his cheek, and bestowed on me an impudent wink as he was led off, it struck me that Benjie was highly delighted with himself or his oratorical display. I failed to see any cleverness in it; I was to think differently later on.

I had been out at Dr Temple's cottage not an hour after the discovery; and as I found the servant perfectly recovered, and with not a scratch to show as the result of the attack, I rashly concluded that she herself was the thief, with or without an accomplice. My idea was that the lying in the lobby with the door open and apparently insensible was a mere feint to throw suspicion off herself while her companion escaped with the booty. My only wonder was that she had not been found bound and gagged as well, and it was that omission which made me wonder if she had done the whole thing single handed. With this thought uppermost I searched the whole cottage and garden very carefully, expecting to find the plunder there buried or hidden. The dog kennel already noticed stood on feet, and was about four inches off the ground, and it seems strange to me now that I did not have it moved or looked below. However, the oversight—which I actually made—mattered little, for at that time the plunder was not there. I merely mention the fact to show what a narrow escape the girl made, for had the stolen things been got there she would certainly have been arrested; and that they were not there found was not through any planning or skill of the thief. That which complicated the case to all concerned proved a blessing to the servant girl.

Peggy Reid, when questioned by me, asserted her belief that she would know the man again who had held the handkerchief over her mouth and nostrils, and stated that she had noticed a man resembling him hanging about the place, and passing and repassing some days before. I had no faith in her ability to do so, for at that time I strongly suspected herself; but I made a raid among "my bairns," and picked up two fellows, who were shown to her without success.

She was positive that neither of them was the man, and they were liberated. If Benjie Blunt had been at liberty I might have thought of him, but at that time he was demurely picking oakum in Calton Jail to wile away the tedium of his sentence of seven days. He had been carried into the Central Office, dead drunk, an hour before the robbery was reported, and what could be more satisfactory to us? Candidly, the thought of Benjie in connection with the singular and daring robbery never once rose in my mind.

Failing with the two first arrests, I kept my eyes open for the spending of the money which had been the chief part of the plunder. A flutter of interest quivers through the whole thieving community the moment a big haul is taken by any of their number. It will not hide; you see it in their faces, in their manner, in their gorging and drinking, and in a certain indescribable furtive uneasiness and excitement which they show when visited and questioned.

The only one whom I found to be unusually flush of money was a man named Pat Corkling, better known as "Pauley." Pauley was more a beggar and tramp than a thief; and had got his nickname by evading hard labour during a sentence for vagrancy by pretending that he had a "pauley," or paralysed, right hand. Pauley, then, was spending money freely, and yet always too drunk to go out begging. I therefore removed him to the Central, and had him searched.

We found more money on him than he could account for, but none of it could be identified, and Peggy Reid, on being shown Pauley, declared most positively that he was not the man.

Pauley was therefore released, and went away triumphant, with the money in his pocket, to resume his drinking and gorging.

At this stage of the affair there occurred a most singular and unaccountable event. Benjie Blunt was set at liberty, having duly served his term of seven days, and that very night the policeman Bain, on the beat past Dr Temple's cottage, was suddenly attacked in a ferocious manner by a man who ran off the moment the assault was made. Since the discovery of the robbery Bain had been ordered, with Dr Temple's permission, to enter the garden by the gate during the night, and make the circuit of the cottage to see that all was secure. He had done so on that occasion, and was scarcely out of the garden when a powerful hand drove the hat over his eyes, while a powerful foot administered a vicious kick to the small of his back. While he was dropping to the ground in agony a voice growled out something to the effect that he was to "take that, you thief!" Bain managed to spring his rattle; but when he scrambled to his feet again he found himself alone, the nimble assailant having flown like the wind. No arrest was made, though Bain had to get a substitute for the rest of the night, and go home to bed.

Next day, as if to add to the complications, a note was handed into the Office addressed to me, with twopence of deficient postage to pay, and which ran thus—

A blake Sheep. yul finde the rober of mr temples is thee Peg on the bete. serche him an his howse an yul see. giv him 10 yers the vilin.

The most of this precious epistle was written in a species of half-text, which did not seem altogether unfamiliar to me. So impressed was I with the idea that I went over to the prison and had a look at the copy-books of most of those in the school or who had been in it lately. I did not come on any resembling it, and it was not till Benjie Blunt came up to me on the street a few days later that the possible connection between him and the curious writing flashed upon my mind.

"Now, I remember—Benjie used to write a hand something like that," was my thought when he addressed me, and I fully expected that Benjie's first words to me would have a reference to the policeman Bain, a most sterling and tried man, in whom we had implicit confidence.

Benjie took a long time to work round to the subject upper-most on his mind, but at length he said—

"I know you're always on the look-out for hints, and you're so kind and attentive when I'm in your hands that I couldn't help coming to you with what I've found out."

I grinned unfeelingly into his solemnly puckered-up face.

"O Benjie, try that on somebody else," I rejoined, with a look which must have convinced him that I was wide awake to his clumsy flattery. "Out with what you've to say; I'll find out your motive afterwards, if it's of any importance."

"What's it worth to put the thief in your hands?" he asked with cunning look, which could not possibly be described on paper.

"It's worth about as much as the thief or yourself—nothing," I calmly answered.

Ah, well, he was sorry for that, but he was still anxious to help us—virtuous Benjie!—and would not mind doing a good action for once.

"You know Pat Corkling? Pauley, they call him," he continued.

"Why! is he the man?" I cried in surprise. "I had a letter accusing Bain, the policeman on the beat, of the crime, and I strongly suspect, Benjie, that that letter came from *you*."

Oh, no, it was quite a mistake. Benjie protested strongly—a trifle too strongly—that he had never written such a letter in his life; and I immediately concluded that he had written that letter, but was puzzled to think why he should now come to me accusing Pauley.

"How do you know that Pauley did the job?" I asked, when Benjie had done protesting.

"I didn't say he did, and I'm not going to say it. I'm not to appear as a witness in the case at all, mind—that must be the agreement, or I tell nothing."

"All right; I agree to that; go ahead with your story—I daresay it's a lie from beginning to end, so it doesn't matter much."

Benjie smiled delightedly at the compliment, and proceeded—

"When I got out of quod and heerd of the thing—which had been done when I was in—I had a idee that the peg was the man that did it, just like the man, whoever he was, that wrote to you," demurely observed Benjie. "Pegs is an awful bad lot—except you, of course—oh, honour bright, except you," he added, catching himself up barely in time. "But then I found out that Pauley had been flush of money for near a week, and I took to watching him. I didn't get much out of him, for he's fly, I tell you."

"That's a great compliment from you, Benjie—what a pity he can't hear it," I remarked.

"But there was some Indian ornaments took, wasn't there?" Benjie added, suddenly coming to the point, and looking inno-cently anxious for enlightenment.

"Yes."

"Well, I saw Bell Corkling with one of them—at least I think it would be one of them—a silver thing, made like a butterfly— and I heerd that others saw her with more, which she had put away in a safe place. O Jamie! ye had Pauley up on suspicion— why didn't you keep him while you had him?"

"That's a mistake which may be easily rectified, if we can find any of the things in their possession."

"Trust you for that, Jamie," said Benjie, in servile admira-tion, at the same time giving me a poke in the ribs for which I did not thank him. "And, mind, be awful suspicious of him if he tries to prove a *nalibi,* as they call it," he added, with careful con-cern. "He's an awful liar, and could get others to swear any-thing."

"Ah! he's not alone in the world in that respect, Benjie," I significantly rejoined, "and has no chance to be till the hang-man gets you."

Benjie gracefully acknowledged the compliment, and, after some more advice and instruction, left me.

I knew, from the moment that Bell Corkling was named, that I should have some trouble in getting evidence against them. They had no fixed abode, and generally lodged at a place where dozens besides themselves might as reasonably be suspected of the crime. This beggars' howf was in the Grassmarket, and its occupants had such a reputation for stealing from one another that I scarcely expected Bell or Pauley to be so foolish as leave their plunder about that place. My opinion to this day is that Benjie *did not* see the Indian trinket in Bell's possession, but merely inferred their guilt from circumstances which I shall notice further on. Therefore the task which Benjie conferred on me was much more difficult than I imagined. I had Bell watched for a day by a smart little ragamuffin whom I engaged for the purpose, and then I broke in on them at what I thought was the most favourable moment—about ten o'clock at night. The "kitchen" was full, but Pauley and Bell were in more select and favoured society—the room of the lodging-house keeper, who was helping them to dispose of some bad whisky. Bell looked angry and excited when I appeared and my men closed the door; Pauley looked concerned, and hurriedly said something across the table to Bell in an undertone, when she made a swift motion as if to wipe her mouth with her hand. All that took place while the fat lodging-house keeper was rising, and, in tones of innocent wonder, asking what I sought at such a time.

I had not an answer ready, for I was thinking of Bell's peculiar action, and watching her closely the while; but at length I said pleasantly to Bell—

"I want to know how old you are, Bell." "Then I won't tell you," she fiercely answered.

"I didn't ask you. I mean to find out for myself. You're such a horse of a woman—I want to see if I can tell by looking at your teeth. Come away, now, like a good soul, open your mouth."

Pauley turned pale, and Bell closed her lips more rigidly.

"Sha'nt," she defiantly answered, in a mumble through her teeth.

"Ah, ladies are always shy on that point; I must take you to the Office, and get a crowbar to prize open your jaws," and I got out my handcuffs to fit one on her, when she suddenly made a desperate gulp, and then turned crimson in the face, and began to wave her arms and kick her legs at a fine rate, gasping, and choking, and sputtering, but failing to get the impediment either up or down her capacious throat. She opened her mouth now without being asked, and the chasm thus displayed was enough to frighten the bravest, but she was so evidently in pain, and urgent in her motions, that I made an attempt to relieve her.

Others tried in turn, but at length we had to send for a doctor, who, with a peculiar instrument—like a long bent pair of forceps— managed to bring out of her throat an Indian gold coin. As soon as I had examined the coin, and made some pleasant remarks thereon, which were very badly received by Bell, I asked for the remainder of the plunder, and not getting it, searched the place thoroughly, when I at last found a small paper parcel tied with a piece of twine, and fastened up inside the chimney with a table fork. In this parcel was most of the plunder, including the old-fashioned watch, which seemed not a bit the worse of its smoking. The landlady was loud in her denunciations of my prisoners, and they were good enough to confirm her protests, by declaring that she knew nothing of the hide. Still all three had to trudge, though the landlady afterwards got off with an admonition. It was the table fork which saved her; for it was proved that she had missed the fork days before, and kicked up a terrible row, accusing one of the lodgers of having stolen that useful article.

The arrest, and the manner in which it had been accomplished, seemed to impress Pauley with a more exalted opinion of my powers. He did not know that it was by a mere chance that I entered at the moment when Bell had the Indian coin in her possession, and seemed to think there was something uncanny about me. That was his first impression. A day or two's reflection made him veer a little. He had never told the particulars of the robbery to a living being—even Bell had not been so trusted. How then could I have known that he must be the man? That was Pauley's puzzle, and it led his thoughts insensibly in the direction of Benjie Blunt. He sent for me at last, and asked me point blank if he had been informed on by that worthy. I was a little staggered by the question, and Pauley took me up at once.

"I see it was him that set you on to me and Bell—and there's nobody else could," he bitterly continued. "Well, I can be even with him, for I'm not the real man after all. If you'll undertake to get me off, I'll put you up to the whole plant."

I could make no such pledge, but Pauley's anger was roused, and he had resolved that Benjie should suffer, so he made un-conditionally the following statement:—

"That night when the robbery was done I met Benjie in a public-house in the Pleasance. He pretended to be very drunk, but he wasn't, and I knew it, and wondered what he was after, as I smelt chloroform, and knew he was the only one who could have it about him. He got quarrelsome and broke a glass, and was put out of the place. I didn't stay long after, as I was curious about him. He went along a street or two pretty drunk like, and then got as sober as a judge, and went out very smart to the cottage at the Meadows. The whole job didn't last five minutes, and I watched it all a bit off. When he came out again he had a narrow box in his hands, and he went to the dog kennel and pushed the box in below it, and then bolted. I went for the box, and got it, and bolted too, for I was frightened, seeing the serv-ant's foot in the lobby, and thinking maybe he had given her too strong a dose. I burned the box whenever I got under cover, and hid everything but the money. I heard that Benjie was locked up for being drunk and abusive the same night. He was no more drunk than I am now, but I s'pose he thought he'd be safer in there than out."

This story was too wonderful for me to credit at a moment's notice, but I thought there could be no harm in getting hold of Benjie. I had pledged my word to him that he was not to appear in the case as a witness; his appearing as a prisoner was quite outside of the bond.

I went to look for Benjie soon after my interview with Pauley, and chanced to meet him coming up a close in the High Street, when he graciously smiled out, and seized hold of my hand to shake it warmly, while he thanked me most heartily for so neatly securing Pauley and Bell. He seemed to look upon the capture as a personal favour done to himself. He was shortly to change his opinion.

"I'll go up the close with you," I quietly remarked, turning and accompanying him as far as the High Street. "There are some points in that affair I'm not quite sure of; and I want you to go with me as far as the Office."

"All right, but I am not to appear as a witness," he warningly observed.

"No, no, not as a witness," I assuringly returned, "and, lest anyone should suspect you of peaching, suppose I put one of these on you and take you along on suspicion?"

He looked at me suspiciously, but recovered and grinned out as I snapped the steel on his wrist—

"It's a good joke," he said delightedly.

"I don't mean it for a joke at all," I said, becoming serious. "Really and truly I am arresting you on suspicion."

His whole countenance changed, his jaw fell, and for a moment he stopped walking, and looked as wicked as any human being could look.

"You can't prove anything against me," he at length answered, moving along with me in apparent confidence. "I can prove a *nalibi,* as it's called. I was in Fernie's public-house in the Pleasance all the afternoon, and was put out there drunk, and lugged into the Office long before the robbery came off. I was drunk, but I knew what I was about, and I know I was never near the Meadows."

"Done!" I cried. "Oh, you fool! Why did you say so much? You've convicted yourself by speaking of an *alibi.* It was the only link awanting in the chain of evidence, for I could not conceive why you should pretend to be drunk and then get back to the High Street and have yourself locked up as drunk and incapable. Thank you, Benjie, for your help in this matter. It was all a clever *alibi* you were arranging?"

Benjie emitted one oath, and then became silent, conscious, doubtless, of the soundness of my remarks. An hour or two after he had been locked up, I had Peggy Reid brought to see him, when she unhesitatingly identified him as the man who had held the handkerchief to her mouth on the night of the robbery. This drove the last prop out from under Benjie, and he plaintively asked if Pauley was to be accepted as evidence. Being informed that that was a likely contingency, he thereupon stated that he would prefer to plead guilty, in order that Pauley might suffer along with him. His benevolent intention was humoured, and the three went to the Penitentiary together, Benjie getting the lion's share in the number of years.

Checkmating a Monster

◎

THE MOTHER WAS a lady-like person of thirty or so, but had a haggard and hunted look which made her look five years older; the child she led by the hand was a boy of five or six, somewhat shabbily clad, and as bloodless in the face as his mother. It was her fearful backward look as she entered which first attracted my attention and roused my curiosity, and then, as she dropped breathlessly into the nearest seat, I saw that she had been either running or walking very fast, and looking as scared as if she had just escaped a murderer. She had a fine oval face, with lovely dark eyes, and must have been actually beautiful a few years before. There was also a refinement about her manner and speech suggestive of better days and circumstances than she now enjoyed.

"I was afraid he had seen me and followed me," she incoherently gasped out when she could find breath to speak, "and it is to save my boy I've come. It is long since I ceased to care what he does to me; but surely the life of an innocent child should be spared."

She was so tearfully excited that I took as much time as possible in taking down her name and address simply to give her time to recover. She gave her name as Mrs. Hendon, but I was surprised to find from her address that she was in lodgings in Rankeillor Street—a semi-genteel place in the South side.

"I have him only for an hour," she hurriedly continued, "and half of that is gone already, so there is little time to lose if I must send him back to that monster. I want to know if I must let him stay and be murdered by inches, or if I can take him away and

127

defy his father to touch him or part us? My lawyer says I cannot interfere; but I think there must be a law to save a human life."

"Certainly. Who is it that seeks to take his life?"

"My husband; his father."

"Oh, indeed," and I gave a queer gasp and said no more. The face of my visitor flushed, and her eyes quickly lighted up till they fairly blazed into mine.

"There! I see you are like every one else," she hotly exclaimed. "When a pair do not agree you at once conclude that the woman must be in the wrong. It is shameful, cruel, monstrous! It is killing me!"

I assured her that she wronged me, and that I only hesitated from long experience of the profitlessness of getting between man and wife.

"If your husband ill-treats you, you may charge him with assault, and have him punished; or you may separate from him, or even procure a divorce," I continued, expecting to hear the old story of love and devotion in spite of brutal ill-treatment. But for once I was mistaken.

"I am already separated from him, and he is too cunning to ill-treat me so as to give me grounds for divorce," she hurriedly answered, and then I gasped again, liking the appearance of things less than ever.

"There is not a human being on earth whom I hate and despise more than the man I married, but all your laws have been made by men, and, of course, they gave men the best end of the whip. He wants to get hold of my property, settled upon me by my father when I was married, and I refuse to give it up, and for that miserable three thousand pounds he is now slowly murdering my boy, after getting me out of the way by a trick."

"What trick?

"Just this—and I must ask you not to think of the ugly look of the thing, but simply that I am as innocent as my own child here. After trying to wear out my life with daily taunts and cruelty and neglect, he one day followed me to the house of an old friend, whom I went to consult in my desperation. That friend was a gentleman, and the man I should have married, and Hendon pretended to be frightfully jealous, and to believe that I went to see Mr. Harley for no good purpose. He waited till I came out, and then confronted me and told me that he had good grounds for a divorce, but that, in mercy to me and my boy, he would be content with a separation. A divorce! the hound! well he knew that if he divorced me he would lose every chance of getting my property. A divorce! I would not fear that. I would hail it even as a Godsend, innocent though I am, but that it would sunder me forever from my boy.

"He even hinted to me when there were no witnesses present that if I would give him the property he would give me the boy. I refused, for that would mean starvation to us, and then he said that he would make us both suffer for it; and he's doing it. I want you to look at the boy's shoulders, and then tell me if there is no law to prevent a murder."

While the mother had been hurling forth this speech in her quick impassioned tone the boy had stood with his tearful eyes fixed on her animated face, and with his thin little hand clasped tightly in her own. As she stooped and whispered a word in his ear, he began to unloose his belt and take off the shabby blouse which covered his slender frame. Underneath was a ragged shirt, not over clean, and when that was opened I saw that his shoulders were covered with weals and bruises. It was a horrible sight, and almost sickened me. The boy, indeed, was least moved of any in that room, for he kept tugging at his mother's hand and saying, "It's not sore, ma. Don't cry; it's not a bit sore."

"How did you get those cuts?" I asked, as I helped the child on with his blouse.

"Pa did it," he answered, with perfect readiness. "He said I looked at him, and then did it with a belt."

"Did he do it all at once?" I continued, for some of the marks seemed old bruises.

"Oh, no. He often does it; every day."

"And why did you not tell me about it sooner?" interposed the mother.

"He said he would thrash me worse if I did."

"And I only found it out through him crying one day when I put my arms round him," added the mother, "and when I went to Hendon about it he declared that the child was a liar, and that he had got the bruises by falling off a wall that he had been forbidden to go near. The story carries a lie in the face of it, for Herbert is too timid to clamber upon walls—indeed he's more like a girl than a boy—perhaps because he is so delicate."

"You may safely charge him with assaulting the boy," I suggested, "for any medical man would know at a glance that these wounds were not the result of a fall."

"That would do no good but just hasten the child's death," she wailed, wringing her hands. "Hendon would only be fined, and then would go home and half murder the boy in revenge. No, no! I want to take the boy from him—it's the only safe plan."

I shrugged my shoulders and said nothing, for that was clearly what she had no power to do.

"Even if he were frightened from beating the bairn he would kill him in some other way," she hysterically continued. "He starves him, and sends him out in cold and wet, poorly clad, and with boots that will scarcely hold together, and if I put better ones on him he tears them off and pitches them into the fire."

"Oh, well, that kind of treatment won't kill the boy," I hastened to assure her. "More children are killed with mistaken kindness and coddling than with hardships like that. Look at those gutter waifs about the Cowgate and the Canongate. They don't die, I assure you, and they endure far worse than your boy. Humanity is like a tree, the more you buffet it the stronger it strikes its roots into the earth. Your husband's object is not to commit murder but to frighten you out of your property, and depend upon it, he will not run his neck into a noose."

"You don't know the man—he is too passionate to think of the result, and would have murdered me long ago if he had not had an interest in keeping me alive. Oh, will you not believe me? I tell you he'll murder that child, and then when it is over, who will fill my empty arms? All your regrets won't bring back my bairn; and even though the unnatural monster were convicted and punished, what good would that do to me? No, no; it's now the action must take place. I've set my heart on saving the child, and I shall do it."

She had a dozen reckless plans to propose, even to the running off with the boy and disappearing to some far off land, in which even a tiger husband should not be able to find them; but they were all unreasonable and impracticable. While I had been reasoning with her the time had flown imperceptibly, and the hour in which she was allowed intercourse with her boy had quite expired. She rose in a flutter of dismay, quite sure that the fault would be visited heavily on the child's shoulders, and at that moment just as she was leaving I extracted a reluctant consent to her husband being summoned to the Police court for cruelty and neglect. They then hurried out together and hailed a passing cab and disappeared, while I returned to the office to fill out the summons, and then deliver it in person. Hendon was not known to me, but I had seen his place in Leith Walk; and fancied him to be a man in fairly good circumstances, as he employed one or two men and rented a good house in Greenside.

It might have been an hour later when I reached the house. It was a half-flat in a good stair with bells at the bottom, but there was no name-plate on the door, and I guessed it to be the right one by the screams coming from within—the screams and wild entreaties of a child in great agony and terror. I gave the bell a vicious pull, and there was a slight cessation of the terrible outcry, but no answering of the ring. I rang again, and still got no answer, and then I thundered at the door with my feet and demanded admittance in the name of the law, when at last there was a flutter of feet and some whispering within, and then the door was opened on the chain by a pallid and excited looking servant girl.

"Is this Mr. Hendon's?" I asked.

"Yes, sir."

"Well, tell him I want to see him."

"He's not in just now," she faltered, but the lie was written in her face.

"Take off the chain, or I'll burst in the door; and it'll be worse for both of you if you try to deceive me," I said, in tones which carried conviction with them, and the door was tremblingly opened, and I was invited to enter. I followed the girl into a parlour, and, then said sharply:—

"What were you doing to the boy just now?"

"Me! I wadna herm a hair o' his head," she tremblingly answered with tears in her eyes. "It's the maister that was thrashin' him for bidin' oot owre lang. He's aye beetlin' him for something," she added under her breath, "I'm fair sick o' seein' it."

"Where are they now?" I demanded, loudly enough to be heard all over the house.

The scared girl pointed with a shaking hand to a door opposite, and I crossed the lobby and dashed open the door, to find within the child I had seen so recently at the Central, with his blouse off and the red blood showing through his shirt at the shoulders. He was cowering on the floor on his knees, and close to him stood an insignificant-looking little wretch, not above five feet high, and with a face more like that of a monkey than a man. I had expected to see a man six feet high at least, and with muscles and limbs like a giant, and I was so astonished that I exclaimed in undisguised contempt:—

"Good gracious! are *you* Mr. George Hendon?"

"Yes," he ferociously returned, facing up at me as boldy as a bantam cock, "and what right have you to force your way in here? I've a good mind to throw you out again faster than you came in."

I looked at the creature, and found that he was neither drunk nor joking, and then simply took out my handcuffs, and said to him:—

"I will not waste words on you. I came here to serve you with a summons for cruelty to your child; now I won't serve it at all, but handcuff you like a thief and march you through the streets, a spectacle for gods and men."

He whitened with passion, but made no reply to me. He simply turned his eye on the crouching child and stared at him fixedly. It would be impossible to put into words all that was in that look, though the child evidently understood its dreadful import only too well. The wretch seemed to say with his awful eyes, "So you have been complaining, have you? Wait till we get back again!"

"I suppose you're some dirty beggar hunter?" he sneered, turning to me.

"Exactly—a hunter of dirty beggars," I cheerfully returned. "Just try how these fit you," and I snapped the handcuffs on his wrists.

"It's just to make sure that you don't attack me and throw me down the stair," I brightly continued, as he began to foam at the mouth. "I am really in terror of my life with a powerful man like you, and the boy seems to share the feeling."

"That vile woman, whom I could divorce at any moment, has been prejudicing you against me," he hissed, looking for a moment as if he would raise his handcuffed fists to maul me, "but I'll pay you both off for it. Every father has a right to make his children obey him, and I'll do it though I should die for it. Take me before your Magistrate. I'm ready for you all, and I'll expose that woman, so that she'll never lift her head again."

I made the girl get his hat, and put it on for him, and then with difficulty got the child to stop crying and take my hand, as he seemed to think that I was taking him away to prison or execution, or to some mysterious dungeon in which he would be left alone with his father. At the bottom of the stair, however, the father sullenly intimated that he would pay for a cab, so I was robbed of the satisfaction of taking him through the streets.

At the Central the charge was duly entered, but an hour or two later Hendon was released on bail, when he instantly asked for his boy, who, however, had been sent to his mother for the night, pending the result of the charge.

"It's all right; I'll have him tomorrow," he darkly rejoined, and I saw him no more until next forenoon in the Police Court. By that time he had got an agent to appear for him, a precaution which Mrs. Hendon had neglected, and that agent smoothly stood up and put such a fair face on the conduct of his client that I was inclined to ask myself if what I had seen was only a distorted dream. He plainly hinted that Mrs. Hendon was a person of the lowest morals, who had only been spared from divorce by the noble mercy and mistaken tenderness of her husband, and that the marks on the child were the result of a fall brought about by his own carelessness. It happened, however, that they had not a single witness to support these statements, while we put his own servant into the box and speedily extracted enough from her to ensure a conviction, if any other evidence than the boy's bare shoulders had been needed. The sentence was a fine of £2 and expenses, or fourteen days, and the money was promptly paid. The moment that trifling transaction was over Hendon with ferocious joy reached over and seized the boy by the arm to lead him out of court. Then a scream burst from Mrs. Hendon, and she turned imploringly to the Magistrate.

"Oh, don't let him take the boy away again! He will kill him this time!" she cried in agonised entreaty.

The Magistrate tried to soothe her, and pointed out that Hendon was now under heavy bonds for his good behaviour, but the woman refused to be comforted.

"What good will the bonds do me after my bairn is dead?" she pitifully wailed. "God cannot see all that cruelty or He would not allow it to exist!"

She was led out by force at last, and then Hendon bent over the boy and gleefully whispered:—

"Now if I don't give you a lesson for speaking against your own father! I swear you'll never open your mouth against me again!"

Just then Mrs. Hendon darted across the lobby and wound her arms about the boy, shrieking out that they should never part, and for five minutes the Court within could not proceed for the noise. When at last she was torn off she fainted clean away, and then Hendon made a bolt for the entrance, and disappeared, dragging the wailing child along with him. When the Court was over, I felt myself touched on the arm, and looked round to find at my elbow a drunken wretch known as "Stoorie Tauch"—a man who had been oftener convicted of drunkenness at the Police Court than any other flesher's caddie in Edinburgh. Tauch was a little red-faced rascal, with a habit of hitching his clothes about every minute or so, and was said to be fit to sell his soul for drink or money.

"Yon man Hendon that was fined for beetlin' the wee laddie— is he marriet?" he asked, with a hitch and showing an uncommon eagerness in his eye.

"Yes, you saw his wife in Court as a witness against him," I answered shortly, for Tauch's breath would have knocked a cuddy down, and his hitching was not pleasant.

"Humph, when was he marriet till her?" he grunted, with another hitch which made me wish a broad bank counter between us.

"Seven years ago," I answered with irritation, and wishing to be rid of him.

"Imphm," he slowly drawled. "Weel, she could put him in jail at ony meenit, for he was marriet afore, and his first wife's leevin' yet."

"Good gracious, Tauchie, can you prove that?" I exclaimed, no longer anxious to be rid of him, and utterly forgetting both his hitching and his evil breath. "Who is she; and where's she to be found?"

"Halkerston's Wynd. She's naething to boast o', but she's that man's wife, I ken, for she often gets money frae 'um."

"You're sure she has not been divorced? "

"As sure as death," and Tauchie drew his greasy fingers across his throat to emphasise the oath.

"Can you take me to her now?" I asked.

"'Deed, wull I," he responded, with uncommon alacrity, and then to my utter surprise the man whom I thought the lowest and most brutalised of mankind softly added, "Man, when I saw that puir wee laddie's back in court there I was like to greet, and says I to mysel', 'By —— I'll pit a spoke in your wheel.'"

I could have hugged the horrible hitching wretch, and his breath now seemed sweeter than perfumes from Arabia. Down to Halkerston's Wynd is only a minute's walk, and Tauchie seemed to have no difficulty in finding the house, which, as I had expected, turned out to be a shebeen kept by a labourer's wife, who had once been fined £7 and was bidding fair to be fined a second time. She was known as Maggie M'Guire, and I was therefore surprised when Tauchie said to her the moment the door was opened:—

"M'Govan's no after ye this time, Maggie; he just wants to hear ye say that that man Hendon in Leith Walk is your real husband."

The woman changed countenance, and then tried to put it off with a laugh.

"That was only a joke o' mine, Tauchie," she awkwardly answered. "M'Guire is my real man."

"Ye're a leein' witch," said Tauchie, calmly, "and if ye dinna tell the truth I'll ca' the heid aff ye!"

She persisted in saying that she had been married only once, and that to the labourer M'Guire, but then Tauchie took her in another way. He told her what he had seen that morning in the Police Court. The woman was melted to tears, and when Tauchie had finished she exclaimed with energy:—

"I am Hendon's wife, and I'll show you the lines, and let you do what you like to him."

"But are you not married to M'Guire?" I asked, fearing we might have a double case of bigamy.

"Oh, no; I'm not married to him, but he's worth twenty of Hendon for all that," was her cool reply, and then she went raking through one of her drawers, and at last produced a certificate of marriage between herself and George Hendon, dated twelve years back.

From Maggie's house I went to the Registrar's, where the certificate was verified, and then I went out to Rankeillor Street and asked for Mrs. Hendon. My pace was not a fast one, and I found it getting slower as I approached the house, for it is a strange announcement to have to make to a good woman that she has been deceived, and is actually no wife at all; and that, with what she had already gone through, might end her altogether. I found her ill and prostrate, but the moment I began my strange story she started up and listened breathlessly till the close, when, instead of fainting or dying on the spot, she rapturously clasped her hands and exclaimed:—

"Oh, blessed be God if it should be true! I should never, never repine again!"

"It is true, for I have verified the certificate," and as I spoke I placed the paper in her hands.

"And I am free to take my bairn from him and go where I please!" she cried, almost delirious with joy, starting to her feet and pacing the room with flushed cheeks, and eyes perfectly radiant.

"Yes, because the boy will now be considered—" and then I stopped, with the dread word on my lips.

"Illegitimate? I know, but what do I care for legal phrases if I get him all to myself, never to be sundered again. I can bear anything now if they only give me the boy."

I drew a long breath of relief, and told her to get on her things and accompany me then and there to Greenside to claim her own. Then for the first time a shadow appeared to strike across her joy, and she paled and let her arms drop helplessly by her side.

"Oh, if we should be too late! if he has killed him! There was murder in his eye when he took him away. I feel—I feel a presentiment that something has happened; that I am never to see him again in life."

"And will you stand here paralysed while he is in danger? "I asked, and the words had the effect of rousing her to action, though she continued to whisper her fears during the drive to Greenside, and was so pale and pinched looking when the cab stopped that I thought she was to faint there before we could get up the stair. Strangely enough, the first thing she did on getting into the stair was to stop and listen intently, as if for the screams of the child. All was still as the grave, however, and we got to the door, when I gave the bell a ring that might have waked the seven sleepers. Hendon himself opened the door, having thrown out his servant, box and all, an hour before, and he seemed utterly taken aback by the sight of us.

"Where's my bairn?" cried the mother, trying to rush past him into the house.

"You're not to see him," sullenly answered Hendon. "He's sulking in there, and pretending he has a headache, and won't eat his dinner. It's just spitefulness——"

"He's dying! I know it! Feel it!" screamed the mother, staggering back, ready to faint.

"Nonsense!" I cried, and hearing a whimper in the room opposite, I dashed in and found the boy fevered and bruised, but not dying or anything like dying.

When he saw his mother he ran to her like lightning and cried out:—

"Oh, take me away, never to come back to him!"

Hendon would have interfered, but by that time I had him charged with bigamy and handcuffed. The shock seemed to deprive him even of the use of his venomous tongue, for he uttered not a word while the overjoyed woman, clasping her arms about the boy, fluttered down the stair to the cab, without a single backward glance at her nightmare. Hendon went to prison for two years, and then disappeared, and Mrs. Hendon has now a much bigger family, being married to the "one she should have married."

"Larks!"

◉

I HAVE REPEATEDLY had occasion to show that none are more liable to be imposed upon and cruelly robbed than thieves, just as those tiny creatures that trouble the uncleanly are found, when examined under a microscope, to be similarly afflicted in turn. But who is to guard the unhappy thief? who is to detect for the hard-working scoundrel, who at much personal risk has possessed himself of some one else's property? Alas, the thief has never been provided for; he is forced to essay the new *rôle* of hunter instead of hunted himself; and the result, as I will here show, is not always a success of dazzling brilliancy.

Among the many cabs rushing down to the Waverley Station, one busy Saturday in June, was one bearing a common brown painted wooden trunk. The box was not big, but it was heavy, as the railway porters found when they hastened to help the cabman to put it on the luggage truck in waiting. The cab itself contained only a young girl, having that unmistakable boldness of manner which stamps the owner as belonging to the shady side of life. The girl knew nothing whatever of the box or its contents beyond the fact that she had been in a roundabout fashion engaged to see it safely to the Railway Station. On the lid of the trunk was tacked a card bearing the words—

P. BRIMMER,
Passenger

and this legend being manifestly incomplete, the porters tuned to the girl to ask what station the box was to be ticketed for.

"Dundee—be sure you ticket it for Dundee," was her reply,

and she was careful to wait by the truck till the thin yellow label was securely gummed on the lid of the box immediately below the ticket. She then disappeared into the booking office, after paying the cabman, leaving the trunk to be stowed up with piles of other boxes, and finally hurled down to the platform for "Fife and the North," for transference to the luggage wagon.

The whole of this common-place scene had been witnessed from a sale distance by a person dressed like a working man, and trying with indifferent success to assume the air of an honest toiler about to change the scene of his labours. This man—who, among many *aliases*, owned those of Pete Brimmer and "Slotty"— the last being acquired by a comic habit he had of slotting people with a knife when he was hard pressed—no sooner saw the girl vanish from the booking-office in the direction of the stair up to the North Bridge, than he carelessly sauntered past the luggage truck into the booking office, giving a passing glance, as he did so, to ascertain that the luggage label was right for Dundee, and then took his place within the ticket rail and duly booked himself third-class for Dundee.

What I hinted as to the minute biters being themselves subject to be bitten will now recur to the reader. No sooner had Slotty vanished from the booking office in the direction of the platform, than a man who had been bending over a time-table at the window immediately above the drawer containing the luggage labels, slipped out towards the luggage truck bearing something in his palm which he had drawn across his tongue a moment before. The whole of the porters were busy with other matters, and, while bending over the truck as if to make sure that *his* luggage was all right, the stranger managed to deftly clap another yellow label on top of that already affixed to the brown trunk. He then turned calmly to the booking office, took out a ticket, and made his way down to the train with the crowd, being careful to slip into the first carriage that came to hand.

In crossing the ferry to Burntisland, Slotty was careful and concerned enough to look in the big luggage trucks for his trunk, and saw an end of the familiar brown box peeping from under the tarpaulin cover. When he reached the other side, therefore, and saw these trucks brought up by horses from the steamboat, he gave his luggage no further concern, but took his place in that part of the train for Dundee, with a deep sigh of satisfaction at having got away from Edinburgh, and out of all danger, so securely and successfully.

Meantime the box had reached the platform of the Burntisland Station, and stopped there, being legibly labelled "Burntisland." Among the last to come up from the boat was the man who had manipulated the labels and he, after a visit to the refreshment bar, which lasted till the train had gone, came out with great importance, and went poking about the pile of luggage, saying—

"Brimmer—Brimmer—isn't there a box of mine in the truck? Ah, there it is—that brown one, porter—thank you!"

The man thus claiming the box was shabby and disreputable looking enough, but what suspicion could the porters have of a man who was almost the last to claim his luggage, which in turn bore the name he had given, and was labelled for that very station? The luggage being duly surrendered, the next question of its new owner was how to get it conveyed from the station. Some would have simply waited for the next train, and gone on to Perth, or some other distant town, but this was too transparent a movement to suit Mr Bob Nailer, otherwise the "Sheffield Blade." After some inquiries at the station, from which it appeared that Mr Nailer had come across to Burntisland for a change of air, he was directed to a furnished lodging a short distance from the station, and after a visit to the house in question he employed a man to convey thither the box, and a carpet bag which he had carried in his hand. The lodging was exorbitantly high in price, as it was near the beach, and the best time for visitors was at hand, but as that was nothing to a man who did not mean to pay for them, there was a charming absence of haggling over terms. The Sheffield Blade was delighted with the lodging, and the landlady was delighted with her lodger—more especially when his heavy baggage was brought in and carefully stowed into the bedroom. As soon as Mr Nailer had paid and dismissed the porter, he found that he had inadvertently left home without his keys, but was lucky enough to find one in the landlady's bunch which opened the brown trunk. He remained shut in the room, with the door snibbed, for a full half-hour after being so favoured, at the end of which time he appeared with the carpet-bag—which before had been light and flat, but was now somewhat distended— in his hand. He had some business to attend to throughout the town, but would be back to dinner, which he ordered with much nicety and epicurean exactness. He then vanished from the house and the town as effectually as if he had quietly loaded his feet with weights and dropped himself into a deep hole in the Forth. The carefully prepared dinner got leave to simmer and frizzle itself into useless fragments, and the landlady began to be thankful that the trunk was left behind—containing, as she ascertained the moment her new lodger left, some wearing apparel and other articles of some value, and not merely a heap of stones, or a couple of screw-nails fastening it to the floor.

A little later in the day, Slotty arrived at Dundee, and turned to the luggage van in pleased confidence to receive his trunk, and was petrified to find that no such trunk was there. Then he swore horribly, and said that the Railway Company would have to pay for the loss, and plainly hinted that the missing trunk contained valuables for which he would not have accepted a hundred pounds. No amount of reasoning could convince him that such valuables could scarcely be called personal luggage, and that therefore the Company could not be responsible for their loss—damages to the full amount he expected, or the box returned.

At first a suspicion prevailed that by a mistake the trunk had been sent to Perth with the other half of the train; but a telegram to that city speedily proved that they were mistaken, and that no such box had been in the Perth luggage van from the time of parting at the junction. The inference was clear—the box must have been left at some of the stations on the way. Slotty, for reasons that will soon appear, objected to informing the police of his loss, and at once elected himself his own special detective, and, so far as his first movement was concerned, did not do badly in the new character. He took the first train back in the direction of Edinburgh, inquiring sharply at every station on the way for a brown painted trunk, bearing the name of Peter Brimmer, and labelled for Dundee. In this way he progressed as far as Burntisland, where at last he was rewarded with a clue. Then his rage knew no bounds, and he swore with such heartiness and appalling zest, that it was evident that he considered thieves the pests of the universe, and fit only to be strung up on the spot when discovered. The porter who had taken the box to the lodging was easily found, and Slotty was soon standing before his box, which he unlocked only to go black in the face with indignation and anger. He danced about like one insane, tore at his short-cropped hair—harmlessly, of course—and finally declared that he was a ruined man—that he had been robbed of watches and jewellery amounting to about £150, and that he would hold the railway responsible for the loss. The means by which the robbery had been managed were patent to the eye, for there was the Burntisland label on the box-lid, and underneath they speedily found the proper one for Dundee. Slotty, in all his passion, was careful to announce his intention to take away such of his property as had been left; but to this the railway officials fortunately objected. Slotty's appearance was not prepossessing; a robbery had been committed; it was just possible that he was not the real owner; they would take possession of the box and its contents till an investigation was made. Slotty declined to leave his address, and when pressed to do so, gave a fictitious one. Possibly his reason was for the moment unhinged: certainly he went out muttering, and stamping, and grinding his teeth as energetically as ever confirmed maniac was fit to do; and to understand the drift of his mutterings, it is necessary to here insert the thoughts which were not allowed to reach the ears of the railway men.

"After me acting fair and square with him, and dividing fair, to cut up treacherous like this! Why shouldn't I go back to town and just slot him for it? I'd like to, and he deserves it, but then he'd p'r'aps kick rip a row, and turn round and peach, and send M'Govan or some of them after me. No, that wouldn't do. Oh, Tommy! if I had yer this minit, wouldn't I give it you sweet?"

Nor was revenge the uppermost or most troublesome thought in Slotty's brain. The firmness of the railway people in detaining the box had added to his other troubles a wholesome concern for his own safety. Among those articles which the thief had thought not worth burthening himself with, was a little claw-footed electro-plated salt-cellar. There were also some bundles of nickle spoons and ivory-handled dinner knives, which appeared not only never to have been used, but never even unfastened. Now, the changed luggage-label clearly indicated that the robbery had been planned in Edinburgh; it was not unlikely that the Edinburgh police would be called in to investigate; and to his bitter regret Slotty now recognised the folly of having affixed his own name to the trunk. After crossing to Granton, pondering these painful points, Slotty, instead of paying a visit to his late companion in crime, Tommy the Twister, otherwise "Apple Jelly," and forcibly presenting him with the blade of his tobacco knife, thought proper to trudge on foot to Leith, and there get into hiding as quickly as possible.

Exactly what Slotty had anticipated occured. The robbery of the trunk was reported at the Edinburgh Central, and the moment the electro-plated salt-cellar and ironmongery goods were mentioned, I conceived a sudden desire to look at the box and its contents. Only a few nights before Slotty's trip to Dundee had been made, a pawnbroker's at the south side had been broken into, and watches, jewellery, electro-plate, and cutlery, part of an ironmonger's stock there deposited, had been taken, to the value of nearly £300. There were clear traces of two men at the job, but up to that moment no clue had been got either to the men or the stolen property. It happened, however, that I was out of town when the welcome news came, and before I returned, a note had been sent in for me by the kindly and well-doing Slotty. "Der M'Govan," he said, "i have to tel you that they pawnbroker's was dun by Apple Jelly—you now who I mean, just tommy, the Twister; so take him as sun as you plese. i will give you more facts by an by. one as nows."

Neither Slotty's handwriting nor his face were known to me very well, but it was different with his late companion. He was an old bird, whom I had limed a dozen times—a cunning rascal, with a liking for malingering in prison, and who had got his nickname from affecting illness approaching to death in appearance, and then, when asked if he had a wish for any particular dainty, opening his rigid teeth to say, "Gi' me some apply jelly."

When the note betraying him as the burglar came to hand, I had, therefore, as little hope of laying hands on Tommy as I had of catching the moon. I felt certain that there had been some quarrel, and that long before I could get near him he would be miles from the city. It was with no little surprise, then, that on going down to his favourite public-house, I found him deeply intent on a game of dominoes, and looking as calm and unconcerned at my entrance as if he had never fingered a pennyworth that did not belong to him.

"Take a hand, Jamie?" he said graciously.

I declined—I had not time, or inclination, and, besides, I was there on business.

"The fact is, I want you," I said at last, seeing him slow to take alarm.

"Me? me?" he echoed, in the most absolute surprise, dropping his ivory cards with a rattle on the table'. "What for?"

"The pawnbroker's," I lightly answered, getting the spare link of the handcuffs ready.

Jelly looked too much overcome with mystification and surprise to make an answer, though he quietly held out his dirty paw to be fastened to my own, and bade his companion good-bye in a tone that showed a foreboding of more than a day or two's detention.

The idea of treachery on the part of Slotty never for a moment occurred to him. They had had no quarrel—they had worked harmoniously and successfully together, and had parted the best of friends after fairly dividing the spoil; so how could he look for treachery in that quarter? Besides, Slotty had not a reputation for double dealing—though his skill with the tobacco knife aforementioned and his passionate disposition made him rather a dangerous companion. No; after a swift thought in that direction, Apple Jelly put Slotty aside, and tried to speculate as to what other loose screw in his arrangements had brought his wrist within my bracelet. While he is thus puzzling himself and accompanying me from the public-house at eleven at night, after the manner of a real story teller I must ask the reader to go back a few hours, to follow his faithful friend Slotty in another of his brilliant ideas.

Slotty had been somewhat precipitate, as we have seen, in jumping to the conclusion that Apply Jelly was the traitorous thief. His detective powers indeed were woefully impaired by his passionate temper, for he never once thought of questioning the lodging-house keeper as to the appearance of the thief; or the subsequent movements of the same gentleman. He simply got into hiding in Leith, and then after brooding over his wrongs sent in the note to me. But as soon as the note had been despatched, another brilliant idea came to him like an inspiration.

They had divided the spoil fairly, Slotty deciding to take his share north to Dundee, while Jelly put his away in a hide of his own, pending negotiations for its purchase with a Glasgow fence. Well, seeing that Jelly had robbed Slotty of his share, what could be better than if Slotty, as soon as Jelly was in my clutches—which would be in an hour or so after the receipt of the note—should pay a visit to Apple Jelly's hide; and quietly possess himself of that gentleman's share? It was even possible that in so doing he might get back his own, which would exactly double his profits. Besides, the beloved Twister was in all probability booked for a longish sentence—there being a superstitions idea among my "bairns" that the touch of my bracelets always is followed by a conviction of some kind—and so would not need the valuables in question. The note was sent to me in the morning, and, rashly reckoning that I had received it, Slotty waited only for darkness to put his plan into execution. The days unluckily were long, but before dusk Slotty was up in Edinburgh and prowling round the den of Apple Jelly—a garret in a narrow close near the top of the Canongate. Some cautious reconnoitering satisfied him that the Twister was from home, though that the garret was not empty he had ample proof in a deep snoring which greeted his ears whenever he got close to the door. Apple Jelly's wife was within, sleeping off the effects of a two days' carouse. This woman was one of muscle and weight, her arm being nearly as thick as Slotty's body. An encounter with her was the last thing he could have wished for, but delay would be in the highest degree dangerous, as Slotty might himself be arrested, or the plunder might at any moment be removed. The room was nearly dark, and the door unlocked; the woman would probably lie like a log if she were not actually kicked into wakefulness. Slotty determined to venture in. Slipping off his shoes and noiselessly raising the latch, Slotty stood within the room, while the great mountain of flesh snored on. The door was reclosed, and then he applied himself to the opening of the hide on the opposite side of the room. This hide consisted of that part of the sloping roof shut off near the window by a low partition of lath and plaster. In this partition an ingenious door had been fitted, made of lath and plaster, so as to give forth the same echo when sounded, the whole being concealed by having pasted over it the lively horrors of the *Police News*. The removing of this covering cost Slotty some work, but at last the door of the hide was open, and the arm of the intruder eagerly thrust into the aperture.

To his intense disappointment he touched no box or bundle of jewellery. He groped madly about—further and further, till he lay sprawling and sweating on his face; with his arm up to the socket in the hide, swearing rapidly in an enforced whisper all the while. Then a new thought came—the hide was long and deep, he himself was slender to a fault—he would go inside and make a thorough search.

He wriggled in at the narrow hole—he got inside—he groped and crawled through every inch of the stifling hole—and then, if he had been gifted with invention, he would have sworn with greater rapidity than before. The hide was absolutely empty! Perhaps one or two of his exclamations, more unguarded than the rest, had reached the garret and disturbed the peaceful slumbers of Apple Jelly's wife. At all events, Slotty had scarcely put out his head at the door of the hide and wedged himself into the narrow doorway, with the intention of wriggling out again, when the gigantic woman started up, and in a dazed way stared round the room. The light was dim, but it was nevertheless good enough to reveal the head and shoulders of a man protruding from a place more sacred to the occupants than the garret itself. With a sharp cry of anger and alarm the strong woman started up and seized the first weapon that came to hand, which chanced to be a strong earthenware dish, which she brought down on the protruding head with a force that, had the weapon been stronger, must have smashed the skull into fragments. Something had to give way, and fortunately for Slotty it was the weapon, which was shivered by the blow, but not till it had inflicted on Slotty a concussion that made him sprawl in a frog-like way on the floor, too much stunned to be able either to speak or escape. Before he could recover, he was dragged up with one jerk of the muscular arm; and though he was then recognised, he was, in spite of protests, kicked all round the room, and finally carried out of the garret and along the passage, and then precipitated with much zest down the worn and cork-screw stairs.

"Wait till Tommy gets back from Mackie's," said the woman as a parting warning, alluding to the public-house in which Apple Jelly was at that moment showing such surprise at my visit, "and he'll give ye twice what I've give ye."

Poor Slotty! if ever a man had cause to feel angry, it was he.

Injury had been heaped upon injury, and now insult and threat were added. When he became sensible enough to sit up, and groaningly feel his sore bones and aching skull, will it be wondered at that his first feeble effort was to get out his beloved tobacco knife?

"Jelly isn't nabbed yet—he's down at Mackie's, and M'Govan's been slower nor usual—I'll nab him!" was his vengeful remark, as he deliberately unclasped the knife and began to sharpen its point on the stone steps upon which he was seated. It is clear that Slotty was far too hasty ever to make a good detective.

As soon as he was satisfied with the keenness of the point of his knife, and able to stand upon his legs with some firmness and without his head swimming at every step, Slotty left the stair and close, and made his way to Mackie's public-house. As he was about to cross the street and enter, I appeared at the door with Apple Jelly fastened to me by the wrist, and in his haste to duck into an entry out of sight, Slotty forgot his intention with the knife. As soon, however, as he found that he was not pursued his rage returned; and seeing that we passed up an adjoining close to avoid' the commotion of the open streets, Slotty dived into the close in our wake. When we were near the top of the close, my prisoner suddenly staggered against me, as if he had been jostled from behind, and cried out—"Somebody's hurt me! I think I'm stabbed!"

At the same moment a rush of footsteps down the close caught my ear, and I distinctly saw a man running; but Jelly's next remark roused some suspicion in my mind that the whole was a plan for escape.

"There he's running, Jamie—loose the bracelet and after him!"

"And lose you at the same time?" I remarked, with a knowing look. "No, thank you."

"But I'm stabbed! Oh! if I didn't know better, I'd swear this was Slotty's work. It's just his style."

I still thought he was shamming, and insisted on his walking out into the High Street; but after one or two groaning steps he dropped on the pavement, looking horribly ghastly, and piteously declaring he could walk no further. I had him carried up to the Office, where an examination speedily showed that he had been stabbed in the side—the knife having actually passed into the flesh, and, after glancing against a rib, passed out again in front. It was not a very dangerous stab, but as it bled profusely at both holes, Jelly soon looked more pale and death-like than he had ever seemed while affecting illness in prison.

Next morning my first business was a trip across to Burntisland, when the moment I read the address on the lid I exclaimed—"I believe that stab was from Slotty, after all." The articles found in the trunk—always excepting the greasy rags which Slotty owned as clothing—were easily identified as part of the stolen property, and, apart from the stabbing altogether, I now began to have a strong wish to find out Slotty's abode. Leaving that task to others, however, I began where Slotty had foolishly left off, and traced the real thief—the Sheffield Blade—out of Burntisland and right along Fife as far as Stirling, by the watches and other stolen articles which he had left in his wake at fabulously low prices. The traces vanished at Stirling, and I suspected that he had there taken train for either Glasgow or Edinburgh. As the former was safest for him, I telegraphed to Johnny Farrel for information, and quickly got word that the Sheffield Blade had been seen in Glasgow trying to form a Watch Club at one of the factories, and would probably be heard of in a day or two.

This was all I wanted, and, leaving him to Johnny, I returned to Edinburgh. By this time Jelly's wife had been allowed to visit the wounded thief in prison, and had given him a full account of her encounter with Slotty, at the same time telling him that that esteemed pal had somehow imbibed the idea that Jelly had robbed him. My arrival with the news of the Sheffield Blade's sharpness supplied a clue to the mystery, more especially when Jelly remembered that Mr Nailer had on one occasion feigned helpless drunkenness, and so overheard some of the two burglars' whispered plans for the disposal of the property. Had it not been that a mere mistake in the address, and some carelessness in packing Jelly's share of the stolen property had led to its recovery in the keeping of the Railway Company at Glasgow, it is very probable that Apple Jelly would not have been nearly so frank in his admissions; but rage is a powerful auxiliary of the detective, and in his heat he now longed for but one consummation of joy—the capture of Slotty.

I tried my best to gratify him, but for many weary days could find no trace of him. I did not believe that he had ventured out of the city, and at length turned to Apple Jelly for advice. He thought for some minutes, scratching his grey head pro-foundly the while, and then eagerly shouted—"Larks!"

"Larks? what do you mean by that?" I exclaimed, not sure but Jelly wished to have one with me.

"Oh, Slotty's mad about larks, and never lives without one or two. Look for larks, and you'll find Slotty."

I thought the advice worthless. I did not believe that Slotty would trouble with his pet hobby while lying in hiding, and still less did I believe that I could find him by "looking for larks;" but though the task was a long and weary one, I did find him in the end, and by that very clue. After many a disappointment, and many a prowl after the keepers of larks in Edinburgh, I one day wandered down to Leith, and was passing through a narrow street running from the Kirkgate, when I heard the painful and wild song of a lark in captivity. I looked everywhere for the lark, but could see none, but by ascending a common stair, I at last got a glimpse of the roof, where I not only saw the lark in question, but Slotty himself seated in his shirt sleeves at the open window, with his heels tilted up and a pipe in his mouth. I did not trouble to shout across, but got down to the street very quickly, called a man from the next street, and went up and politely asked him to put on his coat, after opening the door without troubling to knock. Slotty made a dart for his tobacco knife, which lay on the window-sill ready opened as he had left it after cutting his tobacco;

but I was too well aware of his weakness in that direction to let him get near it.

I tripped him up, and while he sprawled on his face, wrenched back his paws and snapped the steel bracelets upon them before he could get out half-a-dozen of his favourite adjectives.

When he became calmer, I took occasion to reproach him for trying to turn detective, when his powers so manifestly did not lie in that direction, at the same time explaining how egregious an ass he had made himself in regard to Apple Jelly. Then his rage was transferred from me to the Sheffield Blade, and he plaintively requested an interview with that gentleman as soon as he arrived in Johnny Farrel's keeping from Glasgow. This request we thought prudent to refuse, as also the joint wish eagerly tendered by him and Apple Jelly, that they might all three be placed at the bar together—with the Sheffield Blade in the centre. They were tried separately; and when Slotty retired with "ten years" ringing in his ears, he was heard to say that he would live it out just to be even with the Sheffield Blade. The affinity of great minds was shown half-an-hour later by Apple Jelly expressing himself in words almost identical. Sheffield Blade, however, was sent to a different prison to complete his sentence; and regarding him and Slotty I have more to say in another sketch.

The Diamond-Ringed
Apprentice

◎

W E HAD GOT hold of a woman "smashing," or passing
base sovereigns in the High Street, and ran her in to
see what she had about her. Of course we were disappointed. The woman had either pitched away all the "sinker"
she carried, or, what is more likely, carried but one coin at a
time, going back to her store, or getting a fresh one from some
watchful satellite as she slowly changed the base gold into sterling silver. She professed to be very indignant at the charge, and
said that we should hear from her lawyer in an hour or two; but
as she had an English accent, and that brazen look which always
stamps the professional criminal, we could afford to smile at the
threat—the more so as she could not say where she had got the
coin, and declined to tell how she lived, or whence she came.

As the case stood at the close of her examination we had
absolutely no evidence that was likely to convict her; and it was
unlikely that any other of the base coins would come in, as they
were beautifully executed copies, which might have deceived
even a bank teller, and would probably circulate unnoticed for
some time. But the woman had spoken of sending a message to
her husband, and employing a lawyer, and it instantly struck me
that I might make something of the admission. Down I went to
the draper whom she had attempted to victimise, and from him I
learned that the woman had been seen speaking to a man—
respectably attired in a brown overcoat and tall hat—shortly
before entering the shop. The two had held a council of war,

indeed, immediately in front of the windows, which some of the assistants had been dressing out. If I had but known this at the time of the woman's arrest, I might have caught him lingering in the wake of the crowd, or hanging on for signals from the prisoner, but there was no time to fume and fret over the loss. I must act promptly or lose him, and possibly the woman too.

At that time there was but one qualified law agent who had the run of the Police Court cases, which are considered beneath the dignity of a respectable solicitor—though this gentleman had more cleverness in his head than many a half-dozen of these put together. The hint or threat of the woman regarding "a lawyer," instantly directed my thoughts to this agent, whom I may call Mr Bellamy, and it struck me as not unlikely that the prisoner, during her conveyance to the Office, had telegraphed to her accomplice an intimation that he ought to seek the assistance of this sharp-witted gentleman.

I daresay little over an hour had elapsed between the arrest of the woman and my appearance at the office of Mr Bellamy; yet the moment he caught sight of my face and heard me say—

"Was there a man here dressed in a brown top-coat and tall hat?" he laughed outright and answered—

"Aha, Mr M'Govan, you're too late this time! The man has been here and has engaged me to defend his wife; but I have sent him off in double-quick time to where not even you can ferret him out."

"Imphm! That's your opinion, of course—or what you're paid for saying—but I may be excused for thinking different," I dryly returned. "Did he pay you?"

"Did you think I would trust him?" laughingly returned the agent, taking out his purse and producing a sovereign for my inspection. "I am too old a bird for that."

I snatched up the coin and examined it with great eagerness, the lawyer smilingly watching me the while, and then returned it to him in silence.

"Did you think for a moment that I would be fool enough to take a dummy?" he asked, with aggravating pleasantry. "No, no——"

"There is honour among thieves," I said, finishing the sentence for him.

"Ill-natured, of course, because you've lost your man, and will lose the woman too," he coolly retorted.

"You're sure of that?"

"Quite. I mean to get her off," was the confident reply; and as I knew he was not given to boasting, I mentally gave the woman up as lost.

"And will a sovereign pay you for all the trouble you will have?" I snappishly inquired.

"If it does not, I shall get more."

"Oh, then, you know where to find the man?—you've got his permanent address?" I pursued, trying hard to look innocent.

His answer was a knowing wink.

"It's no use, Mr M'Govan, with me," he at last observed. "Just take your defeat quietly, and hope for better luck next time."

"I'll get them yet," I said, rather savagely.

"Oh, well; through time you may; it's the fortune of war," he carelessly returned; "only this time you're done."

I could not admit that, and, agreeing to differ, we parted. The next morning the woman was placed at the bar of the Police Court, and charged with uttering base money with intent to defraud; but Mr Bellamy was there to make a pathetic appeal on her behalf, in which he stated that there was not a particle of evidence against the "poor woman," and so worked on the feelings of the Sheriff that she was discharged with a caution.

It happened, however, that we had been busy with the tele-graph wires during the interval; and just as the agent was leading her out, a man arrived from Glasgow with a warrant for her apprehension on a similar charge.

"Not defeated yet, Mr Bellamy!" I triumphantly exclaimed, as I again laid a hand on her shoulder.

"Let me see your warrant," cried the quick lawyer, and then I knew we were done as the warrant was for Lanarkshire alone, and to get another would take an hour at least.

"Tuts, that's a trifle which we can remedy in a few minutes,"
I said impatiently; but then the agent defied us on our peril to
detain her a second longer, and we were forced to let her go.

The moment the woman was free she called a cab, by her
agent's instructions, and drove down to Leith Railway Station,
where she took out a ticket for Galashiels, which she paid for but
did not use. Before the train started she had quietly slipped out
of the station and tramped to Granton, where she took passage
across the Forth, and vanished by a roundabout route in the wake
of her husband. I was at the Railway Station two hours later with
a proper warrant, and then telegraphed to Galashiels and every
station on the way in vain. She had effectually thrown us off the
scent, and we had just to grin and bear it.

But as yet the case had only begun, for the most extraordinary
and mystifying part of it was to come.

Mr Bellamy, among his other employments, acted as a collector of bad debts, and thus had at times a deal of money passing through his hands which was not actually his own. Not long
after the escape of the woman, a client of his, who had just got a
considerable sum through Mr Bellamy's agency, was paying the
same into the bank, when the teller checked off no less than
three sovereigns from the sum, which he declared to be counterfeit. The gentleman could not believe that they were bad, and
took them back to Mr Bellamy, who was equally hard to convince. He tested them by ringing and a close ex-amination, and
then slowly admitted that they were spurious. He then took them
back to the person from whom they were received in payment,
but this man roughly declared that he knew nothing about them,
but that they were not the coins paid away by him, which were
not only good gold, but much older and more worn than the three
produced. The solicitor was greatly enraged, and had he been
anything but a lawyer, would doubtless have made a law case of
it. How the business was settled I know not; but some time after,
in paying some court fees for a client, Mr Bellamy was again
checked passing a bad sovereign. This time he was well laughed

at, and chaffed so sorely that he was glad to take back the coin and say little about it, though he professed to be thoroughly mystified as to how it could have come into his possession. He was almost certain, he said, that he had got the coin among others at the bank, in getting gold for a five-pound note; but as he could not prove it, was forced to bear the loss. Still another case occurred, by a client presenting two of the bad sovereigns at the same bank, which he said had been paid him by Mr Bellamy; and this time the bank authorities, becoming suspicious, not only retained the coins, but consulted me. Mr Bellamy, from constantly appearing for the defence of criminals, had not the best reputation in the eyes of these gentlemen. What was 'to hinder him, when he had all the sources at his command, doing a little crime on his own account? That was how they put the case to me, and in spite of many an old grudge, I should have laughed at the insinuation against the solicitor's character, had it not been for one apparently trifling circumstance. The coin tendered by the female "smasher" was still in our possession; and remembering my own suspicions of the retaining fee of Mr Bellamy, I turned to this, and found that in date, make, and appearance, the detected coins exactly resembled this original counterfeit. The coins, I may here say, were obviously not the work of a novice— they were so carefully got up and finished, that they could not have been sold wholesale at less than five shillings each. It was quite clear, indeed, that they were the work, not of one man with a few rude tools, but of an expert gang, commanding every appliance for their evil trade.

After a good deal of consultation, I thought I would go down and see Mr Bellamy at his office.

The moment the solicitor saw me, he said—

"I could swear I know what has brought you." "Out with it, then." "Bad sovereigns."

"Yes; what do you know about them?"

"I know absolutely nothing but that they are being palmed upon me in some mysterious fashion which beats me to fathom," he said with great earnestness. "I have just found one in my purse, and I have three in my desk which were checked the other day."

"But it is not these I come about," I quietly observed. "How did you know I came about that?"

"I don't know—I just read it in your face, I think," he carelessly answered. "What is it? Some more I've been paying away?"

"It is;" and then I told him of the coins being stopped at the bank, and how I had been called in.

"That's because H——, the head of that branch, has a pique at me," he angrily remarked, when I had finished. "But never mind— I can afford to laugh at him. But I think you have a theory of your own. Out with it, plump and plain, and I'll be as candid with you."

His manner was so unlike that of a guilty man that I ventured to comply, and bringing out the coin of the female smasher and those checked at the bank, I pointed out that they were identical in make and finish. As soon as I had done so, he took one from his purse and three from his desk, and compared them closely, and said—

"You're right—they're all from one die and one manufactory; but how on earth have they got into my possession?"

"That's just what I want to find out," I gravely answered. "Have you never heard from those two smashers since yon?"

"I have, once. They were rather grateful, I suppose, to me for the neat way I tugged them out of your clutches, and they sent me another fee as an extra."

"Oh, indeed? Was it paid in gold?"

"It came to me in the form of a Post Office order. I thought that was your line of search; but I've been too careful to get swindled in that manner. Besides, it is not two, but perhaps twenty sovereigns which may have been palmed on me. How could it be done? I tell you it's a mystery to me."

"Are you quite sure of the people you got the money from?"

"Oh, quite. There's no doubt whatever about them; besides, to let you into a secret, the bad money has been brought in not from one person, but from several."

"By you?"

"Oh, no; I don't bother with that. My oldest clerk, John Lyle, does that."

"Then he must be the criminal."

"That is absolutely impossible," said Mr Bellamy, with slow emphasis.

"Why?"

"Because, in the first place, he is an old and tried man, of staunch integrity; and, in the second place, there is no possibility of him knowing anything of the makers of these coins. When the man was here, Lyle was at home ill."

"You are sure you never mentioned these queer clients of yours to him, 'or got him to write a letter to them?"

"Quite; and the address is not even written down. I carry all these delicate matters in my head."

"How is it that such a shrewd and trusted fellow has been twice taken in with bad money?"

"I don't know—neither does he—though he is greatly distressed about it. It's a mystery to us both, and if you clear it up, I'll promise never to laugh at you again."

"That's very kind of you," I said, with a bit of a sneer. "Perhaps the laughing will be all on my side. What would you say if I took you away with me on a charge of uttering base money?"

"It would be a great joke," he answered.

"Not to you," I returned, with more seriousness than he had shown. "Really, mind you, I don't know but it may come to that. I'm bound to grab at somebody, and can't be blamed for taking the one nearest my hand."

"Now, don't be spiteful, for if you are you will certainly do something foolish. Take the one nearest your hand, certainly, but first decide who he is. It is not I, for you can see that I have been the chief sufferer."

We talked in this strain for some time, during which I learned that John Lyle, the trusted clerk, often brought in quite a large sum after banking hours, and consigned it to the safe till next morning. To this safe there was but one key, and this, along with some others, remained in Lyle's possession by day, and was handed to Mr Bellamy at night. Upon some rare occasions, however, Lyle took the keys home with him.

I had no particular thought in view in laying bare these facts; but one significant discovery came out of the inquiries—all the money which had been found to be base had been in the safe; not always for a night—sometimes for but an hour or two—but in every instance the coins had come out of the safe cash drawer. Lyle was an old and experienced cash collector, and careful to a fault in examining the money tendered him to test its genuineness. How, then, came it that real gold, or gold supposed to be real, no sooner went into the safe, even for an hour, than it became spurious? It was the old story of the philosopher's stone reversed; it changed base metal to gold, the safe not only changed gold to base metal, but, more wonderful still, changed it into coins manufactured in a certain secret mint in England, the locality of which was known only to Mr Bellamy. Frankly, I may say at this stage, in spite of his coolness, I thought the solicitor the guilty one. I decided, it is true, to see the Fiscal and the Superintendent before taking action, but I felt almost certain that he would be in jail in a few hours. But just then an incident so trifling stepped in to save him, that I almost hesitate to put it down.

I had gone into the front office with Mr Bellamy and examined the wonder-working safe, and questioned John Lyle at the same time; when the office door opened, and a young whipper-snapper of a clerk came in with a cigar in his mouth, a cane twirling in his hand, and a diamond ring flashing on one of his fingers. I thought he was a customer or client, till I saw him place his monkey-headed cane reverently in the umbrella stand, hang up his hat, and take his place at a desk, after loftily tossing the half cigar into the fire.

"A fast youth that," was my mental comment, as I returned to the back room with Mr Bellamy. Just as I was passing from the one room to the other, an idea struck me which made me start and for a moment stand stock still in the doorway. I think Mr Bellamy noticed the curious look, and was about to inquire into the cause, when I stopped him by closing the door and saying in an undertone—

"Have you any more clerks coming in?"

"No; why?"

"Could you send that young lad out for a moment till I test something?"

"Certainly;" and the order was given accordingly, though not without surprise, and the diamond-ringed gentleman was sent an errand to the end of the street—religiously taking with him his familiar spirit, the monkey-headed cane.

"Now, just one question—did the husband of that female smasher tell you his story in this room?"

"Yes."

"Did he speak loud or low?"

"Pretty loud—I think he is a little deaf himself."

"Good; and who was in the outer office at the time?"

"Oh, nobody in particular; Mr Lyle was absent, ill, at the time."

"Then who showed him in?"

"Oh, just that young lad—the apprentice."

"The fast youth with the diamond ring?"

"Yes."

"He'll have a big salary, I suppose—three or four pounds a-week?"

"Get away, man! what do you think I'm made of? He gets exactly fifteen pounds a-year, and jolly well paid, I think."

"Friends wealthy?"

"Well, no; not particularly; but you know if people will have their sons brought up to a genteel profession, they must be prepared to make some sacrifice for it."

"Seems a smart fellow?"

"He is. He'll be a cute one, I can tell you, when he passes."

"Now, would you be kind enough to call in Mr Lyle; and say

something to him in a tone of voice as nearly pitched to that of your queer client as you can remember?"

With just a dawning idea of my meaning breaking out on his face, the solicitor complied; and Lyle and I changed places, with the door closed between us.

Sitting at the desk used by the diamond-ringed gentleman, I found that I could hear that some one was talking in the next room, and no more; but on leaving the desk, and applying my ear to the key-hole, of course I heard every word distinctly. One significant circumstance during this test did not escape my eye,— the safe, during the whole time I had been in the office, had stood unfastened with the keys hanging from the lock.

I returned to the inner room, and quietly asked Mr Bellamy to go over, as near as possible, all that had passed between him and the queer client during the visit. This he hesitated to do, till I convinced him it was to save himself that I wished for the information, and that without it I might be absolutely helpless. The account of the interview was briefly thus:— The man had come in in a shuffling way, and said vaguely that his wife had got into trouble passing some bad money, and he wanted her got off; to which Mr Bellamy, after receiving his fee, promptly replied by advising him to be off as quickly as he could, unless he knew a safe hiding-place in the city. He then told him to walk to Corstorphine, and there take a ticket for Glasgow; then to get out, not in the city; but the first station from it, and walk the remaining distance, after which he was to cross the city and take train at the first station on the other side, and there make his way to England. Hull was the town he hailed from, and thither he meant to make his way, as the "factory" of which he was the chief partner had its headquarters there.

Of this "factory" or base-coining den he gave a clear and lively description, and then ended by saying that, though for prudent reasons he could not reveal the exact spot on which it was situated, Mr Bellamy could always hear of him, or send word about his wife, by addressing him at a certain house in Hessle Road.

As soon as the account was finished, I primed Mr Bellamy in the part I wished him to play, and got him to send the old clerk Lyle out on business, leaving only our diamond-ringed young friend in the outer office, to which he had returned during the narration.

I found the fast youth busy at his desk, and, carefully closing the door of the inner room, I made for the outer door, and then suddenly paused and listened.

"Isn't that Mr Bellamy calling you?" I said to the apprentice.

"He never calls; he rings," loftily replied that young gentleman.

To which I gravely answered—

"I'm sure I heard a voice; put your ear to the key-hole just to oblige me, and tell me what you hear."

The lad stared at me open mouthed, and then complied, thinking me mad, I have no doubt.

But the moment his ear was pressed to the key-hole, he heard—and I heard too—the astounding words from within—

"If you want to send me any news or any message, address me at 'Ralph Hutchin's, Hessle Road, Hull.'"

As the words fell on his ear the lad's eyes met mine, and in an instant his face underwent a series of flashing changes. First it was red, then white, then red again, as fast as one could have waved a hand before his face.

"What's the matter? what's wrong?" I kindly inquired, seating myself on one of the high stools, and keeping my eyes fixed on his face; but he seemed to have no explanation to offer, so I took out one of the base sovereigns I had brought with me; and quietly holding it up between my finger and thumb, I said to him—

"Here is a bran new sovereign, fresh from the coiner's hands— would you be good enough to take it to the cash drawer in that safe and change it for any old or worn-looking sovereign yon can find there?' See, the keys are in the lock—it'll be quite easy."

The flashing changes in colour ceased on the face as I spoke, and he remained ghastly pale, with beads of perspiration breaking slowly from his temples. Still, he tottered manfully forward, as if to take the coin from my hand and brave the thing out, when I quickly changed the coin for the handcuffs, saying—

"I think I will give you these instead. You can keep your diamond ring on till you get to the Office, but you may leave your monkey-headed cane behind, as it is of no value, and they 'don't use such things in prison."

As I spoke Mr Bellamy came forth with the words—

"Is it all right, Mr M'Govan?" and the mention of the name seemed to complete the effect. The miserable boy covered his face with his hands, and began to howl and blubber like a child ordered up for a caning. He persisted in not confessing, however, though earnestly urged to do so by his employer; so I had to take him away with the degrading symbols of crime on his wrists. At the Office he was searched, and one base sovereign found in his purse of the same stamp as those already detected. Then I went to his home, and, by searching his room very rigidly, I found not only a small packet of the spurious coins, but a brief and business-like "memorandum" from the makers, in which they acknowledged receipt of Post Office order for one dozen of "patent lozenges," which were herewith sent as per order. The moment I read this note, it struck me that I might make something of it. Accordingly, before any noise could be made in the papers about the arrest, and without even trusting a message to the telegraph, I started for Hull the same afternoon, and there spent three days, in conjunction with the authorities and sharpest men on the staff, in laying a trap for the clever coiners. During that time the boy Grieve had come to his senses in prison, and was induced to write a note to the coiners, enclosing a Post Office order, and asking for a fresh supply of "patent lozenges." This note was carefully followed from the letter-carrier's hands to that of a man answering the description given me by Mr Bellamy of his queer client. We could have arrested him there and then, it is true, but we aimed at a bigger haul, and accordingly we had him tracked and watched during the whole of the afternoon, during which he never once went near any suspicious haunts.

At night, however, he was less guarded, and went boldly to a house in an obscure and dirty part of the town near the water' side, which he approached and entered with such caution that we had no hesitation in sending at once for the relay of picked men waiting in readiness at the Central. The den was speedily surrounded and the doors smashed in, when we secured the whole gang but one, who leaped from an upper window sheer down into the water, and so escaped.

The coining implements were taken with them, and among the gang I was pleased to find my old acquaintance the female smasher, who did not seem equally delighted to meet me. But gratitude and criminals are always far apart. The whole batch were tried shortly after, and sentenced to various terms of penal servitude, some handsome compliments being paid to me at the time of their capture. The diamond-ringed lad Grieve was taken up and accepted as evidence against the gang, and thus escaped the punishment for which he had booked himself. He remained in England, and probably changed his name, so it is to be hoped it was a life-lesson to him.

Self Executioners

◎

SEVEN YEARS MAKE a wonderful difference on most of us—not only in our appearance, but our sentiments. Time seems to rub the corners off us, smooth out the furrows of hate, and in some cases replace them by the softer lines of friendship, affection, or love. At one part of our lives some one injures us, and we vow vengeance on him the first time he shall come within our reach. Years pass; the hot rage evaporates; we look upon him first with indifference, then with a pitying smile at his shallow cunning or treachery, and then possibly with a tinge of admiration.

"Slotty," otherwise Mr Pete Brimmer, and his friend "Sheffield Blade," otherwise Mr Robert Nailer, parted for their respective sentences of Ten Years, as recorded in "Larks," with the worst possible feeling towards each other. Slotty was enraged at having stupidly used his tobacco knife on the wrong man; and the "Blade" was enraged on the principle that the injurer is always the aggrieved person, and because he erroneously blamed Slotty for his arrest and conviction. Had they but been allowed ten minutes for friendly intercourse in a quiet cell, with their paws unfastened, and the merest stump of a tobacco knife each, I have to doubt that the country would have been saved a considerable sum, even allowing for a couple of convicts' funerals. It would also have saved me a great deal of trouble and hard work; but only a select few earn their pay without working for it, and from that class I have hitherto been rigidly excluded.

Slotty and Sheffield Blade being professional criminals and old jail birds, at once settled down into the old groove, and became well-behaved convicts, penitent and pious to a fault before the chaplain, and humbly obsequious to warders and turnkeys, and so earned their full share of marks; while I have no doubt many a wretched amateur of a criminal, in for scribbling down some name that was not legally his own, would be rebelling hotly at petty tyrannies or gross outrages, and be thus compelled to serve his full term.

The fact that both convicts, though separated by a county or two, had pursued the same virtuous practice, was testified by them being set at liberty within a few days of each other. Both were human, however, and both had had time to cool down and reflect; and, when they met in Edinburgh, instead of grabbing madly at the nearest weapon, they all but embraced, and spent the first few days of their liberty in friendly carousal. "When criminals unite, let honest folk tremble," says the thieves' proverb in its own peculiar language; and I had no sooner noted the renewed friendship of the old enemies than I said to some one, "There will be work on our hands before long, unless we manage to nip up one of these rascals soon." And I was right. "Sheffield Blade" had as much cunning and planning power as would have stocked a half-dozen criminals; Slotty had determination and endurance for the same number; so what could be expected from the new league but a case as puzzling as it was difficult to unravel? Besides, as I have frequently had to show, an odd chance incident often steps into a case to upset the nicest calculations, and as one appeared in this, it thus, added to the number, puzzled the criminals themselves.

One afternoon a gaudily dressed young girl stepped into a jeweller's shop over in the New Town, bearing in her hand a common silver brooch wanting the pin. But a moment or two before her entrance, two things had happened which had some influence upon the things which followed. The first was that Mr Fairley, the jeweller, had left the shop to go home for dinner, and the second was that a girl had gone into the shop with a basket containing the shopman's "tea." The shopman was thus busy in the back-room over this meal when the young woman entered. The two places were separated by a partition and a door, the upper half of which was filled with obscured glass in lieu of panels. At the moment that the bell of the outer glass door sounded, the shopman was seated with his back to the door of the inner room, and, as he was in the act of swallowing a bite, did not rise instantly to go to the front. When he did appear behind the counter, the girl simply showed him the brooch, said she wanted a new pin put into it, and asked how soon it was possible to do the trifling job. A time being fixed, her name was taken down and a printed ticket handed to her, and then she left the shop, while the man returned and finished his meal without further interruption.

All this was such a simple and everyday occurrence—not excepting the apparent character of the customer—that the man thought no more of the circumstance, and certainly never dreamed of connecting it with what followed. He did not mention it to me or any one, and, if he had, it is scarcely possible that I should have gleaned anything from the statement.

Three or four hours later the shop was closed as usual, and that means that it was made almost impregnable to burglars. At that time the open slots in doors and shutters, with lights left burning in the shops, had not been adopted; but this particular shop, though the stock was not very large, was so well protected, that several attempts to break into it had failed miserably. The back windows were not only heavily barred without, but secured within by steel-lined shutters, the front shop was as firmly secured, and the workshop was below the whole, and accessible only from the shop above.

By a fortunate stroke of luck most of the jewellery had that night been taken from the windows and show-cases, and consigned to iron safes in the back part of the shop; but still enough was left both in the shop and the workshop to afford decent pickings for any one able to gain entrance.

Next morning, when the shop was opened as usual by the shopman already mentioned, in company with the foreman jeweller, there were some signs of confusion and disorder to which their eyes were not accustomed. A number of plated articles were lying on the floor behind the counter, as if they had been disdainfully tossed down by thieves intent on purer metal; some trays of small articles which had not been consigned to the safes had been tumbled out on the counter, and hurriedly weeded of their best contents. With the first glance at the place the shopman exclaimed—

"There's surely not been a robbery? Shut the door, Jim, and put your back against it, till 1 have a look round."

This clear-headed suggestion was promptly acted upon, and the shopman soon returned from below with the news that the place had been broken into, and about a dozen watches, more or less valuable, which had been sent in to repair, had been taken, as well as other articles, to the value of about £180 altogether. There were also distinct traces of skeleton keys having been tried on the iron safes, but without effect. Strange to say, there were no marks as of the powerful crowbars generally used on such occasions on hinges and locks. But the greatest wonder was to come.

The man, in his hurried exclamation, had said that the place had been "broken into;" but a close examination of the whole shop, back and front, and above and below, revealed no trace of any breakage whatever of wall, door, plaster, roof, or floor. The thieves had evidently been in, but how had they got in and out again? That was what puzzled the two first discoverers of the crime, and what continued to puzzle us as soon as we were summoned to examine the premises. I could discover no misplaced bolt or tampered lock; no gap in ceiling or floor; no means of either entrance or exit; yet there were the evidences of their presence patent to every eye. In my suspicion I even examined the chimneys of shop and workshop, only to find that they were secured by being each crossed by a strong iron bar, which no burglar could have removed except with incredible exertion.

To say that I was staggered and puzzled by the case does not convey a full idea of my feelings. I was completely upset and. brought to a stand-still, and may truthfully admit that I never once thought of either Sheffield Blade or Slotty as the active hands in the job.

After a diligent examination of every inch of the shop—including every safe, and case, and shelf—I came to the con-clusion that the place had been entered in the usual way, by using the keys of the place, or fabricated duplicates of those keys. This idea was utterly fallacious, but it is as well to notice it, as it led to a great deal of sifting and searching, for which I had nothing to show. Warned by my experience in another case, I tried to discover some means by which the keys of the place might have been got out of Mr Fairley's possession; and finding that they had posi-tively never been out of his hands even for a minute, I was forced to suspect the man who generally called for them in the morning and opened the shop. The man had already plainly told me that he knew he would be suspected, and altogether conducted him-self so like an innocent man that I was brought to this conclusion only with the greatest reluctance, a feeling in which his em-ployer warmly joined. This, however, did not prevent me from arresting the man and searching his house, as well as making strict inquiry into all his connections and his actions before the robbery. All this active work on my part produced nothing. We found no trace of the stolen articles, no trace of the thieves, and no evidence that the keys had been copied or used in any way. These facts are not very creditable to me, but I give them to show that a detective is not omnipotent. To show, indeed, how grievously I was blundering, and what a simple matter would have put me right, I will here go back and give the facts of the case as they were afterwards revealed.

When the girl entered the shop with her brooch to mend, she did not enter alone, but had by her side the Sheffield Blade him-self. The moment they were within, and while the girl was in the act of closing the door, the Blade squatted down on his knees between her and the door, and close to the outside of the broad counter. When the brooch business had been arranged the girl left the shop, closing the door after her, and leaving the Blade still squatting close in in front of the counter, and therefore invisible to the shopman. When the shopman returned to the back-room to finish his interrupted meal, the Blade wriggled across the floor—still on his hands and knees, and therefore below the line of the window in the door of the back-room—towards a big show-case facing the counter. This case was fully ten feet long, and was fitted with six doors—three below of panelled wood, and three above of plate glass. The upper half was fitted with mahogany shelves, which were covered with plated goods; the lower half was a kind of cabinet, which was stuffed principally with patterns and odds and ends necessary to the trade, but not needed for display. Noiselessly opening one of these lower doors, the Blade wriggled himself into the bottom half of the case feet foremost, cursing under his breath the noise made by his feet among some brown paper at the other end of the case, and then as coolly drawing close the door behind him. This daring scheme was as near being detected at the very outset as any scheme ever was. The inside of the door had no handle or protuberance of any kind, and even by digging his nails into the edge of one of the panels the Blade could not effectually close it. He got the door close, but could not get it "snecked," though he fought till the very sweat oozed from his short-cut scalp. This was a simple difficulty which was entirely unforeseen, and the Blade in the despair of the moment expected nothing less than instant detection, and a return to the penal servitude he had just quitted. Yet even here a singular chance saved him. About twenty minutes passed, and then he heard the shopman open the glass door of the back-room, and show out the child who had brought him the tea. As soon as he had done so the eye of the shopman fell on the unfastened door of the case. The Blade heard him pause in front of it, and gave himself up for lost; but all the man did was to put down his hand, grasp the handle of the door, and shut it with a sharp bang, without once dreaming of looking within, or trying to account for it being unfastened. Another curious chance saved the Blade later in the evening, for Mr Fairley audibly told the shopman to "look in the bottom of the big case" for something, and a moment after countermanded the order by saying that the pattern had been taken downstairs the day before.

As soon as the shop was vacated and locked up for the night, Sheffield Blade, with a long sigh of relief crawled out of his hiding-place, rubbed his cramped limbs, and then seated himself comfortably on one of the high counter chairs, and supped heartily off some bread and cheese with which he had provided himself. Then he explored the shop; cursed a great deal, especially at the inventors of iron safes; and then gathered together as much of the stray jewellery as was worth carrying away.

All that he said must remain unrecorded, but as his disappointment at the locking away of the most of the jewellery was keen, the talking must have been both lively and energetic. He had a decent-sized pile, it is true, but nothing like what he considered a fair reward for such risk and ingenious planning.

But seeing that the cunning robber was hermetically sealed up with the valuables, it may be thought that he was reckoning a little too fast. Of what use would the whole treasures of the Bank of England be to a thief who was as safely locked up as its gold? Let us see. The Sheffield Blade had little hope of getting out of prison easily, but he had made some provision for the plunder. In a recess in the back part of the establishment was a closet having one deep, square window—that is, a hole through the wall, two and a-half feet deep and nine inches square, strongly guarded by one solid bar of iron, sunk deep into the stones. By thrusting his arm up to the socket in this curious little window, the Blade could just show his dirty paw outside and no more. He could telegraph, and grip, and motion, but could at the same time see nothing; added to which was the slight drawback that no article above four and a-half inches in breadth could be passed out.

Punctually at twelve o'clock, by the jeweller's regulator clock, the Sheffield Blade adjourned to the closet, and, sinking his arm

to the socket, wagged a signal in the darkness of the common
green behind. There was a prompt response—the answer of his
faithful friend Slotty being the quick thrusting into his fingers of
a half-mutchkin bottle of whisky, which he drew in and applied in
a luxurious long draw to his lips. This done, he took a gold watch
from his pile, and thrusting his arm up to the socket as before,
wagged it as a signal. Strange to say, there was no response. He
wagged again impatiently and incredulously, as much as to say,
"What! will nobody have a beautiful gold watch, only slightly out
of repair?" He wagged indeed till he was tired, but there being
no answer he was forced to draw in the prize—cursing much in a
suppressed voice as he did so. After a pause he again thrust out
his hand and signalled, when his paw was at once grasped in the
unmistakable thieves' grip. He then tried the watch again; it was
deftly removed; and so he continued passing out the plunder till
the whole pile was gone. He then signalled that he meant to
hand out no more, and returned to the adjoining room to exer-
cise his skill in vain upon the locks of the safes. There were
abundance of hammers and wedges in the workshop below, but
hesitated to use them on account of the noise, and would have
given anything for a strong crowbar, which he had neither been
able to bring with him nor thought of asking Slotty to pass into
him. The few skeleton keys he carried with him were feeble and
useless:, so after an hour or two's hard work he gave up the task,
and proceeded—not to break out of the building, which was impossible, but to prepare for the rest he had so industriously earned.

The sweetest happiness we can enjoy upon earth is to look
back on hard work successfully accomplished. Had the Blade,
then, not the surest guarantee of a sound sleep? Everything soft
in the shape of paper and workmen's jackets and aprons he collected and conveyed to his sleeping place, which was—where
do you think? The case which had hidden him was surmounted
by a broad and deep cornice of mahogany, much like that which
crowns the most of bookcases, and behind that was a proportion-
ately roomy hollow or recess, nine inches deep, ten feet long,

and more than a foot broad. This elevated perch, indeed, could not have suited him better had it been made and planned for his reception. Peacefully the hard-working Sheffield Blade laid his head on his pillow of stolen coats and slumbered till morning, till the very inserting of the key in the front door by the shopman.

During all the alarm and shouts of discovery, the Blade lay listening with the most lively interest, not unmixed with concern for himself. And when I appeared, and began at one end of the place and ended my search at the other, he all but gave himself up for lost. I even, it seems, stood up on a chair to examine *the top shelf* of the case, little dreaming that a few inches higher would have revealed the reclining form of the Blade to my eyes. To look back on the oversight seems idiotically stupid, I admit; but at the time I was not thinking of the thief actually being on the premises, having all but decided that the job was the work of an amateur, not a professional criminal. I completed my examination and left the place, and then the Blade began to look out for an opportunity of leaving his perch. He had fully expected to get such a chance in the course of the day, but the stir and excitement of the robbery brought too many into the shop, and night found him still imprisoned, half famished, and beginning to get seriously concerned. After the shop was shut up, he ventured down, and signalled several times through the closet window, and at last was rewarded by having a parcel of bread and beef, and the indispensable whisky, thrust into his hand by the faithful Slotty. It is possible that Slotty—who had learned a little writing and reading in prison—might have conveyed to the Blade at the same time some written message, but the Blade had not made good use of his various sentences, and could neither read nor write. After another night's rest on the top of the case, the Blade, now grown desperate, resolved to get out at whatever risk. The shop was opened as usual, except that Mr Fairley, who had had new locks put on the door, accompanied his men; and then when the foreman was below, and the shopman and his employer at the back, the Blade was left for a moment with no one in the front shop but an old woman who was busy scrubbing up the floor in front of the counter. By and by this woman worked her way back and round the end of the counter till she was stooping behind; then with a quick scramble and drop, the Blade got down at the end of the cornice next to the door. The sound was instantly heard by the old woman, who looked up with a start, when the Blade nodded cheerfully and said, as he laid his hand on the door latch—

"Nice morning, isn't it?"

He then vanished from the shop, shutting the door so softly that no one heard him go; and having disarmed the woman's suspicions so effectually that she never once spoke of having seen him and imagined all along that he was one of the working jewellers employed below.

Sheffield Blade was probably elated and happy at what he considered the culmination of success; but if so, his joy was brief. He made his way straight to the den of Slotty, whom he found alone—his spouse being then in prison. Slotty was all joy at seeing him, and hastened to prepare breakfast, and then rather puzzled his guest by saying—

"And where's the swag?"

"What?"

"Where's the swag ?" repeated Slotty. "Where did you stow it?"

"Stow it? I didn't stow it anywhere; I handed it to you through the little winder."

"That'll do for you!" said Slotty, with a knowing smile. "Come on now—no gammon; what did you do with it?"

There was a horrible pause, during which each thought the darkest things of his beloved pal, not unmingled with suggestive recollections of the past.

"Do you mean to tell me you didn't get it all through the winder?" said Sheffield Blade, getting livid with passion, and speaking with unnatural slowness and distinctness.

"I mean just that. Soon as I tipped you the bottle I heard a noise behind, and saw a man look out of a stable loft behind the green, and making sure it was a peg, I bolted."

Sheffield Blade said nothing, but got out from the back lining of his coat a leaden-headed "neddy," which he had the reputation of being able to use, and Slotty instantly saw that something was wrong, and apprehensively fumbled for his tobacco knife.

"You think to do me wi' that miserable story?" breathed the Sheffield Blade, with deadly distinctness.

"Strike me dead if I'm not telling the truth," cried Slotty, in earnest protest. Then a sudden light appeared to dawn on him also, and he opened his knife with energy, hissing out the words, "Oh! that's your little game, to do me out of my share? Say you handed it to me through the winder, and kick up a row, all for sake of appearances! Oho! thought because you done me wunst afore, and got me ten years, you'll do me again, eh? I'll just settle up now for this and old scores as well."

Sheffield Blade seemed to have no objections. The ruse of Slotty to appropriate the whole of the plunder was too transparent, he thought, to pass for a moment for the truth, and he acutely set the whole down to chagrin at having agreed that the Blade's share was to be three-fourths and Slotty's only one quarter of the entire proceeds. The table was between them, or he would have used his neddy there and then, but instead he only turned up the cuff of his right sleeve, saying—"Once for all, will you deliver up fair and square or not?"

The reply of Slotty was to snatch up a teapot and hurl it in the face of the Blade, who instantly delivered a terrific blow at Slotty's head, which was as deftly evaded as had been the teapot. Then they slowly circled the table—the one with his tobacco knife, and the other grasping his neddy, till at last Slotty made a dart forward, and made a beautiful slash at Sheffield Blade's arm.

The dig of the knife and the spurting of the blood roused the Blade into action, and he hurled himself across the table at his wiry opponent, bringing the neddy crash down on his head and shoulder. The rest was easy, for Slotty dropped at once—the tobacco knife rolling across the floor from his nerveless grasp, and then the Sheffield Blade had everything his own way. He did his work as effectually as if he had been a paid executioner employed by Government to rid the world of a pest, and shortly after walked out of the place unchallenged, leaving Slotty in a state of insensibility from a fractured skull, from which he never recovered.

Slotty was found thus by some one and carried to hospital, but as no one had been seen near the place, no one was blamed or sought for. No one was at Slotty's funeral, so there could be no tears shed, and nothing but smiles of satisfaction from all he had troubled during his life greeted the cheerful announcement that he was at last beneath the turf.

Sheffield Blade, however, could not get rid of the idea that he was being pursued, and at once got into hiding, the place of safety selected being fortunately a hole beneath the floor of a condemned land, and immediately above a common sewer which had providentially become interrupted in its flow. The consequences might easily be foreseen.

Breathing the horrible air of this hole for some days—eating in it and sleeping in it—he imbibed enough poison to have killed a whole colony of criminals. At the end of the week he felt so bad that he crawled out and said he didn't feel well.

He was taken to the Infirmary all but insensible, and it was then found to be a case of malignant typhoid. Sheffield Blade lingered just long enough to rave out most of the facts I have put down, and then I had a search in one of the stables immediately behind the jeweller's shop, resulting in the discovery of a hide in the loft containing most of the stolen articles.

A groom who kept the keys of this place strongly denied all knowledge of the robbery; but when we found one of the stolen articles in his possession, and two more in his home, he admitted having been in the green on the night of the robbery, whence he had seen a man escape in a scared manner, and having had the articles handed out by some one whom he had never seen or heard of. This story, which I now believe to be strictly true, seemed so utterly absurd to judge and jury when he came to be tried, that they unanimously found him guilty of housebreaking and reset, and awarded him the full penalty of seven years' penal servitude. Who after that will say that a penniless thief like Sheffield Blade cannot bestow a legacy on another?

The gradual revelation of the facts of the case was a sweet morsel to M'Sweeny, especially that part where I was within a few inches of the real robber without ever suspecting it; and to this day, when I have been puzzled, he will give me a dig in the ribs, and say suggestively—

"Och, Jamie, avick—why didn't ye look on the top of the glass case?"

A Cracksman's Ruse

◉

IT IS THE curiosities in crime which bother us most; those in the plain beaten track being prosy and unromantic enough, and often calling for no special skill in their unravelment. If a man breaks into a jeweller's shop in the ordinary way, and carries off part of the stock, there can be no doubt as to his object in making the attempt, and thence by inference tracing the crime to the likeliest pest of the hour who happens to be on the surface. There is a good deal, too, to be gleaned from the manner in which the job is executed, most cracksmen having a style of their own; but occasionally a case arises so incomprehensible, so far removed from the ordinary run, that we make the strangest blunders in the unravelment.

When the case now before me was reported, the first question which arose in my mind was, "What on earth could be the object of a thief in breaking in there?" A lawyer's office in an upper flat in George Street—a simple pair of rooms containing nothing but an iron safe full of papers, some tin boxes, and a case of law books, with of course one or two desks and writing tables—had been in a mysterious way entered and ransacked. There was no money taken, from the simple fact that money was not kept in the place. By accident a gold watch belonging to the owner of the chambers, the glass of which had been broken the day before, had been left in one of the desks, and this was taken, along with an indiscriminately selected heap of papers, of great value to the loser, including some railway scrip only too easily available at its market value. Strangely enough, an envelope containing £500 in bank notes, which had been left with the lawyer by a friend the day before, and thrust at the moment into the breast-pocket of his office coat, was found safe and untouched. The coat was rather a shabby one, and hung on its nail behind the door exactly as it had been left by its wearer the night before. So much for the plunder taken; but a greater staggerer remained in the means by which the burglar had gained entrance. The rooms formed part of a whole flat, kept by a worthy couple above every suspicion, and were not only closed with detector locks, but also guarded by an outer door, which was found in the morning firmly locked and bolted on the inside, with the key in the lock, just as it had been left by the keepers before retiring to rest for the night. Nor did the detector locks show any signs of having been tampered with, though the safe had certainly been opened with skeleton keys, or at least keys not originally intended for the lock. I turned to the window, and found it to be four storeys off the ground, and could not believe it possible for the burglar to bring a ladder of that length and use it without discovery. This narrowed the means of entrance to a descent from the roof; but after an examination of the hatches I was doubtful of even that. They were all secured with padlocks, and all locked, and a burglar does not generally trouble himself to close doors so securely behind him.

Such was the case as it stood, and though there was cause for congratulation, inasmuch as the bank notes were safe, the lawyer was nearly distracted at his own losses, and precipitately proposed to offer a reward for the return of the papers, "and no questions asked." I could not allow that, and merely counselled patience, while I tried my best to trace the stolen property and the skilful thief.

In spite of the state of things left by the burglar, I for some time tenaciously held in my own mind that the robber was an amateur, and also some one connected with the office, and possessing means of admittance suspected by none. Yet I found that by working in this belief I made absolutely no progress; and getting the use of a slater's ladder and ropes, I ascended to the roof and made an examination from the hatch to the edge of the roof; with the result that I found the zinc rhone pipe slightly bent inwards at a spot directly above one of the office windows, as if a rope had been there suspended and heavily strained. Assuming that this had been the means of entrance, I promptly decided that no amateur would have risked his life in this way, with only the tenacity of a few strands of hemp to preserve him from a beautiful smash upon the pavement below. This done, I pondered as to the likeliest man among my own "bairns" to try such a feat, and would have at once plumped on "Fifty-two Tom," had the smallness of the stake not staggered me. It was incredible to me that this man, who had no lack of brute courage, as well as cunning and skill, and a quickness of decision that would have made his fortune several times over in any honest walk of life, should risk so much for so little. Still more puzzling was it to me how he should ever have gone near such a place in hope of plunder; but mystified as I was, I thought it could do no harm to try and see him, and if possible "sound" him on the point. I had tried others without success, and my reasons for trying him were that I was nearly at the end of my tether, and that I knew he had a liking for working a job single-handed, and thus being bothered with no division of profits. The very way in which his odd name was earned illustrates this practice of his. "Fifty-two" was not Tom's prison number, but the number of a shop in the New Town, which Tom persisted in trying to break into. Tom tried it once, and was scared, chased, and caught, and got six months. Then thinking, perhaps, of Robert the Bruce's spider and the lucky number seven, he tried it again, was caught, and narrowly escaped conviction. He was detained, and got two years on another charge, but the very week after his term expired, he tried No. 52 again, and this time had the immortal reward, in the shape of seven years' penal— another illustration of how perseverance and the number seven are eternally united.

To "Fifty-two Tom," therefore, I turned, not very sanguine of success, nor at all hopeful that this very wary old bird would be easily caught with chaff.

I met him in the Canongate one afternoon, strolling easily along with a pipe between his teeth, and he gave me a cool and patronising nod as was his wont. This nod always seemed to me to say, "Ah, you think yourself smart because you took me once, but try me now." I was continually trying, but not with great success.

"I say, 'Fifty-two,' do you know anything of that job in George Street?" I suddenly asked, pulling up and watching his face keenly.

A novice in crime would at once have pulled on an innocent or an ignorant look, and exclaimed, "What job? Never heard of it," &c., &c.; but not so "Fifty-two."

"Lawyer's place—lot of papers and a gold watch?" he inquiringly said in his thieves' Latin, speaking with the utmost coolness.

"Yes."

"I read about it in the papers," he calmly answered. "What of it?"

"You weren't in it, were you?"

"No."

This answer meant nothing. Whether in it or not, of course, I never dreamt of him saying "Yes."

We eyed each other for a moment or two steadily, like two skilled fencers, each wondering what ruse or feint the other would next attempt.

"Those papers are wanted badly," I at length suggestively remarked. "I daresay money might be given for them, if we could get the cracksman along with them who did the job."

"I never betray a pal," said Tom with virtuous severity, after a thoughtful pause, "so even if I could spot the cove, I'd be the last to do it. But the papers might be got," he hastened to add, with some eagerness; but then I had to check him.

"They are of no use without the thief," I coldly remarked; "at least I cannot treat for them, and what's more, the lawyer, Mr Graham, will not treat for them either. We've taken care to bind him to that."

A slight shade of disappointment, it struck me, crossed the face of the wary criminal as I spoke, but he affected the utmost indifference, coolly beginning to cut some tobacco for his pipe, and saying—

"In that case, I should say they'll go into the fire very quick. At least, if it was me, I should do that; but one can never tell what some coves will try."

"No, one can never tell," I echoed, with an unmoved countenance; "but if you should hear of them, you know the way the wind blows—money for them, and the man who did the job."

I did not know it then, but I had given "Fifty-two" Tom subject-matter for deep thought. One more effort I made to get at him.

"What a bungling stupid he must have been that did it," I observed, "to go and pass over £500 in bank notes."

"Very stupid," he said, with fierce energy and a much stronger word for the adjective.

We parted there, and Tom went up the High Street, pondering and planning and scheming over what I had said. "I never betray a pal," meant about as much with him as the "No" had meant when I asked if he had been in the robbery. Its real interpretation was, "As long as I'm all right with my chums and likely to make something out of them, they're safe; when I'm not, let them look out."

Now Tom had a grievance, and he had at that very moment a friend, to betray whom would have given him the sincerest and most unqualified satisfaction. The only difficulty in the way was that Tom's friend did not happen to be the burglar, while he himself did happen to be that very individual. Volumes might be written on the ruptures and quarrels between thieves and fences; each is necessary to the existence of the other; but when it comes to a question of risk, the thief bears nearly all, and so places himself sadly at the mercy of his more cautious ally.

The name of Tom's friend and fence was M'Guire, otherwise "Snapping Andy." Andy had earned this name from a playful habit he had, when in difficulties with the police, of dropping on the ground and snapping at their calves with his teeth He was well known in consequence. A knock or a bruise soon heals and is forgotten; but an inch or two out of one's leg is a more lasting souvenir. The cause of the rupture was simple. On the night of the robbery, and long before it was known to the police, "Fifty-two Tom" had called on "Snapping Andy," at his home and place of business in Leith Wynd, and offered him a gold watch, wanting the glass, for sale. It was a valuable watch—worth at least £20 second-hand—and they both knew it, and could agree on every point but the price to be paid for it. After much argument on both sides, Andy paid down £3, declaring that he had no more ready cash about him, but that he would pay the difference next day. On the following day "Fifty-two" called for the money, but by this time the news of the robbery had got abroad, and "Snapping Andy," having his client absolutely in his power, insisted on Tom showing him the stolen papers, that he might estimate their value and perhaps buy them. This proposal did not meet with Tom's approval, and they thereupon quarrelled hotly; and as a matter of course "Fifty-two" got no more money, but, on the contrary, was plainly told to be off, or he would find himself in my hands.

All this was very galling, and the more so as Tom found himself helpless to retaliate. He brooded over his wrongs, and turned things up in every possible way; but though he had no lack of cunning, there is a limit to the inventive powers even of such a rascal, and he could hit on no feasible scheme until my suggestive remarks gave him the clue to his course of action.

Dropping in at "Snapping Andy's" shop, he once more asked if that gentleman meant to "stump up," adding, by way of casual news—

"I saw M'Govan just now, and he says there's to be a big sum given for them papers."

"I knew there would be," returned Andy, with interest and some excitement. "If you had let me manage that business it would have been done by this time, and the money paid. Every man to his own line, you know."

"I'd be sure to trust you after the watch business," said Tom, with a scowl.

"I will pay you the rest of the price agreed on, honour bright, as soon as I get the money," said Andy, with great gravity. "What more would you have?"

"Nothing—if you do that, it's all I ask," said Tom sceptically; "but you don't touch the papers for all that I have them put away in a safe hide, and I'm keeping an eye on the spot, just to make sure nobody taps my mine. They'll stand lying by for a bit—the price is not likely to get less by holding on to them for a while."

Many protestations of honour and integrity were showered on him by the eager "Snapping Andy," and offers the most tempting added if Tom would but indicate the hiding-place of the papers, and leave Andy to conduct the delicate negotiation with the owner; but to all "Fifty-two" turned a deaf ear.

"I think I know where your hide is," at last remarked Andy at a venture.

With considerable skill "Fifty-two" assumed an alarmed expression and cried—

"Never! Where is it?"

"No matter. Don't be astonished if you find them gone, and the whole thing arranged without you," said Andy, with a knowing look, and wishing to keep up the alarm. "Will you agree to let me work the thing out or no?"

"No;" and with this apparently furious retort "Fifty-two" left the shop, with some show of concern and alarm in his cunning features. Andy watched him from the door of his den, and noting that "Fifty-two's" pace was much swifter and more business-like than usual, suspected that he had really frightened him, and concluded to follow him at a safe distance.

"He's maybe off to see after his hide now. If I can get the least inkling where it is, I can easily work out the rest myself," was Andy's reflection; and as he considered himself the most cunning man in existence, not excepting "Fifty-two," his course was at once decided. Drawing on a greasy cap, and shouting to his wife to look after the second-hand boots and shoes which formed the blind to his real business, he followed "Fifty-two" up the High Street as far as George IV's Bridge, and was more than gratified to find that his friend appeared suspicious of being watched and followed, and was continually looking back. though never as it seemed actually catching sight of the fence. Less cautiously he traversed the Bridge, and got to the head of the Meadow Walk, still apparently ignorant of the fact that he was being followed. It was a fine bright afternoon, though late in the year, and the middle-walk was crowded with people; so Andy had little difficulty in keeping "Fifty-two" in sight without being himself seen. But when the corner of the West Park was reached, there came a change, for "Fifty-two" entered the West Park, and Andy hesitated to follow for fear of being detected. At that time the shrubberies of both East and West Parks were fenced at that part by a high, unsightly wooden fence, instead of the low light iron rail at present surrounding them; and as "Fifty-two" no sooner entered the park at the corner than he turned to cross it almost in a line with the middle-walk, Andy simply walked straight down the centre avenue, keeping a sharp eye on "Fifty-two" from behind this high wooden fence. When nearly across the park, "Fifty-two" suddenly paused within about five paces of a solitary tree which stands there to this day, and looking down on the greensward, appeared to press the turf down once or twice with his right foot, and then passed on, got through the fence at a turnstile farther on, and disappeared.

"Got it, I believe," muttered "Snapping Andy;" and after a pause to allow "Fifty-two" to be well away, he left the shelter of the railings, and crossed boldly towards the tree. There were many children and others playing about, or enjoying a stroll in the park, and Andy was forced from motives of caution not to appear too curious; but he nevertheless managed to discover what he thought was a distinct cut in the turf at the spot which he had seen his friend and pal press down with his foot, and by negligently appearing to lie down on the grass for a few moments, he managed to mark the spot by thrusting into it his own well-worn tobacco knife, and there leaving it, with the end of the haft just far enough out of the ground to be easily felt in the dark. It does not appear what "Fifty-two" was about, or where he was posted during this arrangement, but I have little doubt that he was witness to the whole proceeding from some adjacent coign of vantage.

These delicate manoeuvers over, "Snapping Andy," after noting well the position of his knife in relation to the tree, left the Meadows and went straight back to his den, where he exultantly penned an anonymous note to Mr Graham, stating that he had a clue to where the stolen papers had been hidden by the burglar, and would return them on payment of a suitable ransom. This note was duly received next morning, but as I have now to show, it was by that time of little value. To understand how so much generosity was thrown away, and at the same time illustrate the bitter injustice which at times is meted out to the able and virtuous fence, it is necessary to follow the movements of "Fifty-two" after so unsuspiciously indicating the spot where his plunder lay concealed.

"Fifty-two" walked straight from the Meadows to my house and asked for me. I chanced to be at home, and left the table the moment I heard his voice, pretty sure of what was coming.

"You said money was offered for them papers," he cautiously began.

"Yes, with the man that did it."

"Oh, in course, in course," he readily returned. "Well now, how much might they be worth, with the cove that did it?"

I thought for a moment, eyeing him closely all the while, and then said—

"Twenty pounds."

"It's too little—it won't do," was his prompt rejoinder.

"That's not my fault—it's not I who offer the money," I sharply returned. "Take it or want it."

"I think I'll take it," he graciously concluded, after a pause to consider. "Just write down that I'll be paid that, and put your name to it, and I'll tell you all I've found out."

"I won't. My word is as good as any paper. You must be content with that or nothing."

"Fifty-two" had another grave consultation with himself, and knowing me well, conceded that point also.

"I'm to get £20 whenever the lawyer gets back his papers?"

"Yes, if you yourself have not had a hand in the job."

"Oh, that's settled. D'ye think I'd come and tell you all about it if I was the thief?" he said, with an innocent smile.

"You're bad enough for anything," I snarled, getting impatient.

"Thank you. Your opinion's worth something," he said, evidently highly flattered, and wishing to bestow a little subtle praise on me in return.

"Out with it then—who's the man?"

"I never betray a pal," he repeated, with all the unflinching integrity of a bank director. "I'll tell you how you may nab him and the papers too, but don't ax his name nor nothing. If you get him, good and well; the job is yours, not mine—see?"

I was trying hard to see, but not succeeding over well. Certain that he was dealing double, I nevertheless was far from understanding the whole drift of his words and revelations.

"Well, the papers is planked somewhere in the West Park of the Meadows," he at last ventured to say. "Is there a tree there, standing by itself near the south-east corner?"

"There is," I answered, after a moment's thought.

"Well, it's somewhere near that tree—how near I don't know; but as they're like to be lifted to-night, you can get the spot watched, and see the whole thing for yourself."

"How is that to be done? Watch a spot in the middle of an open park? That's a nice easy task!"

"Oh, that's just the thing you're good at," said the sly rogue. "There's houses on the other side of the walk, with gardens before them, and there's the trees on the walk, and if you're particular to be close at hand, you can go up the tree itself. and just drop on him. Ha, ha! that's good—drop on him when he's lifting the plunder."

"Have you any idea how the job was planned? I mean what possessed the man to break into an empty office in the way he did?" I asked, after a few more questions.

"Oh, yes, I heard all about that," said "Fifty-two," with a beaming artlessness charming to behold. "It was the bank notes he was after."

"Those that he missed? How did he know they were there?"

"Oh, easy enough. He was standing at the bar down at the Theatre, having a glass of beer, when a couple of swells came in, an' began arranging how they would go out that night for a spree. 'But I've got £500 on me,' says one, 'and I might lose it.' 'Oh, leave it with Graham till to-morrow,' says the other; 'he can lock it in his safe for you. Off you go, and I'll wait here till you come back.' He went away to George Street, and the clever cove as I'm a speakin' on followed him, and saw from a painted sign at the bottom of the stair, that Graham's was on the fourth flat. The swell wasn't long there, and then the cracksman he inspected the place, and saw that it could only be done from the roof."

"But he didn't get the money after all?"

"No, that was the d—d—I mean the blasted stupidity of him. And he did give the bottom pockets of the old coat a squeeze too, though never thinking a lawyer would be so careless as put money in his breast-pocket, and leave it hanging there so innocent like; and there they were all the time, more's the—fortunate thing for the lawyer."

"He'd felt rather bad, I suppose, at missing the prize?" I suggested, with a grin.

"Bad! If it had been me, I'd a sworn myself black in the face," said Tom, with energy. "And it wasn't an easy job either. Think of the risk—if that rope had broke, there'd been an end of him."

"Yes; but it would have saved me a deal of trouble, and been a great benefit to the world," I callously remarked—a sentiment from which "Fifty-two" dissented somewhat tartly.

After some further conversation, "Fifty-two" arose to go; but before doing so let fall rather a curious remark.

"I'm the only one that knows about the robbery but himself, and it's possible that if you nab him he may suspect, and then round on me out of spite."

"Very possibly he may."

"But you won't believe him?" he somewhat anxiously continued.

"Neither him nor you—the evidence must speak for itself," I curtly answered, and with this he had to depart content.

It then wanted but an hour of sunset, and I had little enough time to make my arrangements. I sent out M'Sweeny at once to loiter in sight of the spot without himself being seen, and as soon as it was dark followed with other two men, whom I planted much further away than I wished, though in sight of the tree. As for myself, there was nothing for it but to get a "back" from M'Sweeny, and clamber up the tree and seat myself as comfortably as possible among the strong branches.

The night luckily was a dark one; but to prevent accidents I had drawn a crape over my face, and covered my hands with black cloth gloves, after buttoning my coat to the throat to cover every scrap of white likely to show in the dark.

I began to weary of the task, and my bones were aching with the horribly hard seat; but about twelve o'clock I had my reward, for then a man muffled to the ears appeared, and began to grope cautiously over the turf below my perch. After some patient crawling and feeling with his hands, the man produced a trowel, and after a swift look around, began to turn up the turf, and throw out the earth with marvellous celerity. A moment or two sufficed for the task; the trowel struck on something metallic, and in a moment he had tugged out a tin deed case, such as lawyers use, which he opened with a subdued exclamation of delight, revealing for a moment the fact that it was filled to the lid with papers of various kinds. That was all the length I could allow him to go.

With one spring I was down at his back, with my two hands knotted firmly to his throat, carrying him over on his face, box and all, with the impetus I had gained in the descent. Though taken completely by surprise, the man instantly made desperate efforts to wriggle round so as to face me; but I pounded his face deep into the dirt he had thrown out, whistling out sharp and shrill to the others, only too conscious of my inability to hold him long. M'Sweeny was the first to reach us, and the moment his leg was within reach of the wriggling ruffian's face it was seized by the calf in a set of dog-like teeth, and bitten nearly through. M'Sweeny's frightful yell as he dropped on the ground quickened the movements of the other two, and they pinned him by the legs and hair, not a moment too soon, while I pulled back his arms and snapped the handcuffs on his wrists in spite of every contortion and effort he made to elude the steel.

"I'm murdered—I'm kilt!" groaned M'Sweeny. "Begorra, if it's not Snapping Andy ye've got, I'll let him nibble off the calf of me other leg free gratis."

I wrenched the crape from my own face, and the men turning our prisoner over at the same moment, we simultaneously recognised each other.

"M'Govan!" he cried, in abject surprise.

"Snapping Andy!" I returned, even more astonished than my prisoner. "Why, what on earth took you so far out of your own line? I thought fencing paid you too well for you to trench on the cracksman's ground?"

"You don't mean to say I had anything to do with the robbery?" he shouted, with a wonderfully concerned and horrified look. "I can swear I never touched or saw these papers or that tin box before."

"Ay, you're good at swearing," I coolly returned, while the others laughed derisively.

"He'll be swearing next that he hasn't taken his supper off my leg," said M'Sweeny, with a groan.

"I can clear myself—I can prove an *alibi*. I can tell you who it was that did the job," he desperately persisted; then, after a start and a pause, he muttered with a deep oath, "I believe it's all been a trap, and I've been done by that 'Fifty-two Tom.' He's your man. Get him, and I'll bear witness against him."

"It's too late; we've got one man, and that will do in the meantime," I coldly returned.

"You've no proof," he shouted.

"Tuts—and you taken with the box in your hand? Take him away;" and helping up the groaning M'Sweeny, and giving him a lean all the way, we left the Meadows perfectly satisfied with our night's work.

When nearing the Central Office, a shabby figure sidled up to us and raised its hands in affected surprise, and with a growl Andy recognised "Fifty-two Tom."

"What have you took him for?" he inquired of one of the men; and being answered, he appeared more horrified than ever, and in a tone of virtuous reproach exclaimed, "Oh, Andy, how could you try that?—every man to his own line!"

A torrent of furious declamation from Andy followed. He wanted us to seize "Fifty-two" there and then; but that worthy showed his sense of security by coolly entering the Office with us, and adding several statements tending to further implicate Andy. On examining the tin case, I was disappointed to find that everything was there but the gold watch.

"P'r'aps you'll get it down at his shop," suggested Mr "Fifty-two;" "but he's got some patent hides, so it's possible you'll not nose it."

Andy was locked up after making a vigorous and emphatic statement to the effect that "Fifty-two" was the real thief, and then I paid a visit to his shop. This was ostensibly a place where second-hand boots and shoes could be bought and sold, Andy in his prison experience having learnt enough of the art to be able to cobble a little. I searched high and low for the watch; but though I laid bare more than one hide, I found them all empty, and was beginning to fear that the watch had been got rid of in the usual way through some of the export agents, when my attention was attracted to a pair of remarkably heavy boots standing on an upper shelf. The peculiarity of this pair was that one of them was covered with dust, while the second appeared to have been only recently handled and was almost clean. I looked at the boots, felt inside of them, and then turned them bottom up, when I was at once struck with the size of the heels, which were not fitted with iron plates, like the soles, but with a smooth and almost nail-less piece of leather. I looked at the heel closer; and while M'Sweeny held the candle nearer, I tried to pinch and prise at the edge with the point of my knife. As I did so, my eye chanced to light on the scared face of Andy's wife, whom we had roused out of bed to make the search, and in the terrified glance she returned, I read that I was at last on the right scent. Another dig or two of the knife brought the top of the heel clean away, when I found that it had simply been glued on—the heel itself being a hollow box in which was snugly imbedded Mr Graham's watch, glassless, but sound as when it had left his office.

We had now as good a case against Andy, so far as evidence was concerned, as we could have wished for, and he was brought to trial, with his wife, shortly after. "Fifty-two Tom" would have been happy to tender his evidence, but having a strong case we politely declined the offer.

"Snapping Andy" was convicted of the robbery—innocently, of course, but that mattered little—and sentenced to ten years' penal on account of his reputation and previous convictions.

"Ah, Andy, every man to his own line!" reproachfully observed "Fifty-two Tom" from the front row of the audience, as his friend was being led away. "You'll have time to sharp your teeth against coming out again."

"Ay, and a knife too—look out!" was the savage answer; and then he went off to his ten years', and his wife to her six months', while good, innocent "Fifty-two Tom" accompanied me to Mr Graham's, and received the sum of £20 as the reward of virtue.

During the progress of the case I had striven hard to enmesh him too, but Andy's wife unfortunately had not been cognisant of the watch having been bought from him, so "Fifty-two" went off in great elation to squander the £20. Of course I soon had him for something else, and he at his own request was sent to a different prison from that which sheltered his friend Andy. "Fifty-two" was the first to reappear in Edinburgh, but then he was in broken health and had to find refuge in the Infirmary. While he was still there, and making no progress towards recovery, a visitor was one day announced at the usual visiting hour in the afternoon—a man who came into, the ward saying, "Where is my dear friend, 'Fifty-two Tom?'"

Weak as he was, "Fifty-two" sprang up with a cry of terror when he recognised the face of "Snapping Andy". Then before any one could enterpose, Andy's fingers were clenched about the throat of the unhappy scoundrel, and he had him dragged out of the room, across the wide stone lobby without, and then hurled bodily down a whole flight of steps to the landing below. Nor was that all; for he instantly followed up the attack on the senseless man by kicking and worrying him, and then was beaten and mauled and half-killed before he was dragged off. "Fifty-two" was borne back to bed, and ended his days there a month or two after, while Snapping Andy went back to prison, where he one day so distinguished himself by snapping at the calf of a convict's leg, that the man in self-defence slipped off his iron-shod shoe, and gave him a neat tap on the temples, which ended his snapping for ever.

Afterword: "The Mysterious Maister McGovan"

◉

WILLIAM C. HONEYMAN

WILLIAM CRAWFORD HONEYMAN (1845–1919), writer, editor, violinist, and publisher, was born in New Zealand, a grandson of minor Scottish poet and songwriter Adam Crawford. In 1849 the family returned to Edinburgh, where Honeyman received his musical training and later led the orchestra at Leith Theatre, near Edinburgh. His later tours with a Scottish theatrical company provided the background to some of the fiction he contributed to the Dundee-based *People's Friend* from the 1860s.

Honeyman joined the staff of the *People's Friend* and the *People's Journal* in 1872. He contributed a massive amount of fiction and factual pieces, and a "Violin Queries" column, where he answered letters from correspondents, and, for a small fee, would value violins sent to him in the post, and publish the results.

Outwith his journalism, he adjudicated traditional fiddle competitions, performed regularly, and had many works published concerning his real love, the violin—technique, history, practical tutors, and some of his own compositions—as well as the pseudo-autobiographical McGovan series.

Honeyman had six children: five boys who died young, and one daughter, Lisa, who survived him. She continued publishing her father's works, and even after her death Honeyman's *Strathspey and Reel Tutor* is still on sale in Scotland, and his *Scottish Violin Makers* in print, alongside McGovan.

William Crawford Honeyman

JAMES McGOVAN

The fictional James McGovan first appeared in serial form in the *People's Journal* (from 1873) in *Brought to Bay; or, Experiences of a City Detective*, published in book form in 1878. *Hunted Down; or, Recollections of a City Detective*, came out in 1879, followed by *Strange Clues; or, Chronicles of a City Detective* (1881), *Traced and Tracked; or, Memoirs of a City Detective* (1884), and *Solved Mysteries; or, Revelations of a City Detective*

(1888). The books were very popular; by 1884 they had sold 25,000 copies and at least one (*Traced and Tracked*), had been translated into German and French. Two more books, *Criminals Caught* (1921), and *The Invisible Pickpocket* (1922) were published posthumously, while *The Edinburgh Detective* (1883) and *Secret Confessions* [n.d.], possibly two earlier works under different titles, surfaced in the United States.

Honeyman would have had two local literary models as guides when he began: William Russell's invented detective "Waters", debuting in the serial *Recollections of a Police Officer* (*Chambers Edinburgh Journal*, 1849), and Edinburgh City detective James McLevy's successful memoirs *The Sliding Scale of Life* (1861), amongst others. Honeyman copied neither writer, but could have had practical assistance from Detective Sergeant William Osborne of the Edinburgh Police, to whom he presented *Strange Clues; or, Chronicles of a City Detective*, "as a slight tribute to his skill and energy in his profession", in 1882.

Honeyman revealed his McGovan authorship (no doubt an open secret in Scotland) in his signed dedication in a copy of *Brought to Bay* which belonged to the American crime writer, Ellery Queen: "To David L. Cromb this collection of GOOD LIES is given by the author, Wm. C. Honeyman". Cromb, a literary agent, added his own description of Honeyman, who, incidentally, also led the Dundee Symphony Orchestra:

> "McGovan" was a little, bandy-legged man, with a black spade beard; he invariably wore a velvet jacket; his chief interest in life was playing the violin and he was rarely seen without his violin case; his house in Newport-on-Tay [across the river Tay from Dundee] was actually named Cremona.

HONEYMAN AND SHERLOCK HOLMES

A case can be made that Honeyman, as an author and as a musician, influenced Sherlock Holmes's creator, Sir Arthur Conan Doyle (1859–1930). Doyle had grown up in Edinburgh, and was still a medical student at the University when his first published work, "The Mystery of Sasassa Valley", appeared in the local weekly *Chamber's Journal* in 1879. By that time, *Brought to Bay* had appeared in book form (1878), with *Hunted Down* following in 1879.

Conan Doyle is likely to have read such popular detective fiction; indeed, McGovan and his predecessors may have led him towards that genre, although Sherlock Holmes was the intellectual antithesis of James McGovan's sentimental portrayal as "a man who won't be beat". But it is likely that Honeyman, always seen with his Stradivari, and a leading writer of detective fiction, unknowingly supplied Doyle with the idea of making musical sensibilities central to Holmes's character.

The first description of Holmes, in *A Study in Scarlet* (1887), may give the game away: "My companion", Watson recounted, "was in the best spirits, and prattled away about Cremona fiddles and the difference between a Stradivarius and an Amati". Even if Conan Doyle never met Honeyman, he needed only to have glanced at the chapter headings for his *The Violin and How to Master It* (c.1881): "Chapter III: The choice of an instrument—Genuine Cremonas and copies—Leipsic or German Fiddles...." Honeyman's actual influence on Sherlock Holmes may remain a mystery, but the violin was in Holmes's hands from his inception, when Conan Doyle, in his earliest notes, described him as a "collector of rare violins. An Amati..." The final confirmation may be deduced from Holmes's decision to retire to the South Downs and to keep bees, for thus the violin-playing sleuth becomes a "honey-man," as he remains in the final Holmes story in *His Last Bow* (1917), a title which may be pronounced in more than one way.

Mary Anne Alburger

P. S. One more mystery—why is the master of suspense, Alfred Hitchcock, said to have included the plot device known as a "MacGuffin" in all his films? The word was suggested by his Scottish friend, Angus MacPhail, a screenwriter whom he had known since 1926. Is it possible that MacPhail could have been thinking about, and saying, a ... "McGovan"?